"Are you involved with anyone in Eagle Mountain?"

"Isn't the answer to that question already in my file?" Zach asked.

"It isn't," Shelby said. "There's no personal information at all."

"Then why bother keeping a file?"

"We kept track of your whereabouts in case there was any threat to your safety from the Chalk brothers."

"And is there?"

"Not that we've been able to ascertain."

"But you said Camille came here because she thought I was in danger."

"That was what she thought, but we never found any evidence to prove that. Which is one of the most frustrating things about her disappearance. If she had stayed put, both of you would be safe now."

He heard the anger in her voice—and the grief. "Maybe whatever she was worried about is somewhere on her laptop," he said.

She nodded. "Maybe so."

"Will you tell me if there is?"

"If you're in danger, I'll tell you," she said. "Even if I'm not supposed to."

MILE HIGH MYSTERY

CINDI MYERS

Harlequin

INTRIGUE

For Jim. Always.

Harlequin®
INTRIGUE™

Recycling programs
for this product may
not exist in your area.

ISBN-13: 978-1-335-45685-4

Mile High Mystery

Copyright © 2024 by Cynthia Myers

For questions and comments about the quality of this book, please contact us at CustomerService@Harlequin.com.

TM and ® are trademarks of Harlequin Enterprises ULC.

Harlequin Enterprises ULC
22 Adelaide St. West, 41st Floor
Toronto, Ontario M5H 4E3, Canada
www.Harlequin.com

Printed in U.S.A.

Cindi Myers is the author of more than seventy-five novels. When she's not plotting new romance storylines, she enjoys skiing, gardening, cooking, crafting and daydreaming. A lover of small-town life, she lives with her husband and two spoiled dogs in the Colorado mountains.

Books by Cindi Myers

Harlequin Intrigue

Eagle Mountain: Criminal History

Mile High Mystery

Eagle Mountain: Critical Response

Deception at Dixon Pass
Pursuit at Panther Point
Killer on Kestrel Trail
Secrets of Silverpeak Mine

Eagle Mountain Search and Rescue

Eagle Mountain Cliffhanger
Canyon Kidnapping
Mountain Terror
Close Call in Colorado

Eagle Mountain: Search for Suspects

Disappearance at Dakota Ridge
Conspiracy in the Rockies
Missing at Full Moon Mine
Grizzly Creek Standoff

Visit the Author Profile page at Harlequin.com.

CAST OF CHARACTERS

Special Agent Shelby Dryden—Shelby befriended Camille while Camille was in witness security. Now she's tasked with helping to find Camille's killer, but she hadn't bargained on Camille's brother, Zach, making her job more difficult.

Zach Gregory—Search and rescue volunteer Zach Gregory still mourns the murder of his sister, Camille, four years previously. Learning she actually died only a few days ago sets him on the hunt for her killer.

Camille Gregory—After Camille witnesses the murder of a federal judge at a restaurant where she works and agrees to testify against the killers, she goes into witness security to protect herself and her family. Leaving that protection costs her her life.

Charlie and Christopher Chalk—The Chalk brothers run an infamous crime syndicate in Houston, but they were acquitted of the murder of a federal judge despite Camille's testimony against them.

Todd Arneston—The writer claims to be penning a book about the Chalk brothers, but he seems particularly inept at the job.

Janie—The fellow camper may have witnessed Camille's murder, but she seems more interested in seducing Zach than helping the investigation.

Chapter One

The storm-swelled creek roared like a jet engine readying for takeoff as it rushed through the narrow canyon. The normally shallow trickle of water was now a torrent, tearing great chunks of earth and rocks from its banks and carrying broken branches and whole trees along in its wake. On the other side of the cataract, a group of campers clustered around several vehicles, cut off from escape by the rushing water.

Zach Gregory stopped at the edge of the water, alongside his fellow Eagle Mountain Search and Rescue members, and studied the situation. They had to find a way to get the stranded campers to this side of the swollen creek, even as rain continued to pour. He counted at least six adults, several children and three dogs. All of them were drenched. Even in rain gear, Zach felt cold and damp, rain lashing his face and seeping past his collar and down the back of his neck. He moved up alongside fellow SAR volunteer Caleb Garrison. "How are we supposed to get over to the camp?" he shouted to be heard above the din of the water.

Caleb pointed downstream. Zach followed his gaze and leaned forward to get a better look. The creek channel widened into an open area, the water forming a wide pool, the current much less swift. Newly elected SAR captain Danny Irwin motioned for the group to move toward this pool, and they set out, splashing through puddles and slipping in mud and on slick rock as they shouldered the rescue gear they had carried from the nearest road. The main route to the campground was washed out, and the weather had been deemed too bad to risk bringing in a helicopter to airlift the stranded campers. With conditions only expected to worsen, the forest service, Rayford County Sheriff's Department and Eagle Mountain Search and Rescue had decided to attempt a land evacuation.

Away from the swiftest water, the roar dulled enough to make conversation possible. "We're going to shoot a line across to that group of trees over there." Danny indicated the clump of piñons up the bank. "We'll attach instructions for someone on the other side to secure the line. Then we'll send a group over to assess everyone and send them back across, one at a time."

Someone unpacked the chunky, red line-throwing gun, which used compressed air to propel a coil of strong cable across a chasm. Volunteer Ryan Welch handled firing the gun. A crowd had gathered on the opposite bank, and two men ran to retrieve the other end of the line as soon as it hit the trees. They unwrapped the note and sent a thumbs-up signal across, then began fastening their end to the trees, while Ryan and Eldon Ramsey secured the cable on this side.

"Think it will hold?" Ryan asked Danny when the line was secure.

"Only one way to find out." Danny looked around. "Any volunteers to go first?"

Silence as they contemplated the turbulent gray water rushing beneath the thin line. Fall into that, and even with a life jacket, you could be in trouble.

"I'll go." Zach stepped forward.

Danny looked him up and down. "I guess if the line will hold you, it will hold anyone," he said. "Get suited up, and we'll give it a try."

Five minutes later, fitted with a helmet and personal flotation device, Zach slipped a harness over his hips, clipped onto the line and grabbed hold of the strap attached to a pulley on the line. Tony Meisner clapped him on the back. "Ready?"

Zach barely had time to nod before Tony pushed him and he was sliding down the line across the water. The cable sagged beneath his weight, and he felt spray from the churning water splash onto his legs as he skimmed over the creek. But the cable held. If not for the driving rain and heavy pack on his back, it might have been a fun trip, like riding a zip line on vacation.

Two men rushed to greet him as he landed on the opposite shore and helped him off the line. The radio attached to his shoulder crackled. "I'm sending Hannah and Sheri over next, so get ready," Danny said.

Paramedic Hannah Richards and former captain Sheri Stevens arrived in quick succession. They were greeted by a growing crowd as additional campers gathered beside the creek. Zach followed Sheri and Hannah into a chaos of wet and anxious campers. Dogs barked, children cried and everyone seemed to be talking at once. Everyone was muddy, wet and frightened. "We woke up, and there was water running through our tent," one man told Zach. "My oldest boy left the tent to go pee, and he almost fell in the river."

"There's a tree down on an RV at the back of the campground," another man said. "I think someone might be hurt."

"My husband was hurt by a falling branch," a woman said. She hefted a toddler on her hip. The child—a girl, judging by the pink barrettes in her hair—stared at Zach, her thumb in her mouth. "He's over by our trailer, but someone needs to look at him."

Hannah keyed her radio. "We've got some terrified kids over here," she said. "And some of the adults aren't in much better shape. Apparently, a tree came down on an RV, and there may be injuries or people trapped inside. We've got other injuries from falling trees. We need people over here to administer first aid. And a couple of people to ride with the kids back across wouldn't hurt."

"I'll send people over, and we'll start the process of getting people over to this side," Danny said.

"Zach, start gathering people who are ready to get out of here," Sheri said. "Make sure they know they've got to ride across that line, so only a small backpack or a bag they can carry in one hand can go with them. Everything else has to stay here."

"I can't leave my dogs," one woman wailed.

"We'll get the dogs out, too," Sheri said.

Ten minutes later, Zach was sending the first of the campers back across the line. As the woman started across the water, Hannah approached Zach, carrying a blanket-wrapped small child. "This is Micah," she said. "He's three, and he's suffering from hypothermia. I've tucked some hot packs in around him, but he needs to get to someplace warm and dry ASAP. I'm sending his mom right behind you." She put the child into Zach's arms.

Zach stared down into a pair of frightened brown eyes. Micah had his thumb stuffed into his mouth and said nothing, though tears—or maybe raindrops—slid down his flushed cheeks.

"It's okay, baby." A petite woman, dark hair plastered to her head, stood on tiptoe and stroked Micah's face. Then she looked up at Zach. "Don't drop him," she said.

Zach tightened his grip on the child. "I won't."

Traveling back across the river was much slower than the original traverse, since it required being towed uphill by volunteers on the other side. Halfway across, Micah began to squirm and wail. Zach held tight and tried to talk soothingly, though he was terrified he would drop the squirming child, despite them being clipped into safety lines He sagged with relief when fellow team member Carrie Andrews stepped forward to take the boy from him, then he stepped to one side a few moments later to allow Micah's mom to reunite with her son.

The next hour was a blur of traveling back and forth across the flooded creek. The rain stopped and the sun came out, and Zach began to sweat in the heavy rain gear, but it was too much trouble to divest himself of pack, life vest and harness, so he left everything on and focused on the work. He carried another child across, transported medical gear and escorted a frantic, snapping golden retriever who was determined not to be harnessed to anything. Zach was only able to get the dog to cooperate when someone produced a packet of beef jerky, which Zach fed, bit by bit, to the trembling dog all the way back across the water.

After the dog, there were only two more adults to get back across, and they didn't need Zach's help. He shed the harness and layers of gear and drank a bottle of water someone handed him. A tall blonde woman he hadn't seen before, one of the campers, he supposed, moved through the volunteers. "Thank you so much," she said to each one. When she got to Zach, she took his hand. "You were amazing."

"I was happy to do it," Zach said. It felt good to help other people, to make a difference.

She smiled, showing dimples. "I'm Janie. What's your name?"

"Zach. Zach Gregory."

"Well, Zach Gregory, you and the other volunteers are real heroes," she said, then surprised him with a hug.

He stepped back, a little embarrassed but also pleased. He hadn't joined Search and Rescue for the adulation, but who didn't like to feel they had done something good for someone else?

"How is it you rate a hug and all I get is a handshake?" Caleb grinned at Zach after the woman had moved away.

"I guess I'm just lucky."

"Right. I'm sure that's all it was." Caleb punched him in the shoulder, then moved on to help gather up their gear.

Zach bent and picked up his harness, helmet and rain gear. At six foot four and 230 pounds, he was used to attracting attention, and women seemed to like his looks, but he preferred to stay in the background.

"You did great out there today," Sheri said as she

joined him in collecting gear. "You stayed calm, and you kept everyone else calm."

"Thanks." This was the kind of praise Zach preferred—for the job he did, not for how he looked.

"Uh-oh." He and Sheri both turned at this exclamation from Ryan. Across the river, Hannah, Eldon, Deputy Jake Gwynn and Forest Ranger Nate Hall stood around a fifth figure on the ground.

"Jake and Nate went to search the RV that was damaged by the fallen tree," Sheri said. "They must have found someone hurt."

They hurried to join Danny, who was on the radio. "We'll send a litter over," Danny said. "Secure the body, and we'll bring it over."

"Is there a fatality?" Sheri asked when Danny ended the transmission.

He nodded. "I don't have any details. Jake and Nate found her near a van hit by a fallen tree."

While some team members prepared to bring the body to this side of the creek, Zach and the others gathered their gear and escorted the rest of the civilians up the trail to the road, where sheriff's deputies and Forest Service employees, along with a few of the campers' relatives and friends, waited to drive them back to the town of Eagle Mountain.

They were packing up to leave when a solemn procession came up the trail—Ranger Hall, followed by Jake, Eldon, Hannah and Danny with the litter bearing a wrapped body. They stopped beside the Search and Rescue vehicle and lowered their burden. Sheriff Travis Walker, in muck boots and a yellow slicker over his khaki uniform, came to meet them. "What have you got?" he asked.

"Her ID says her name is Claire Watson, from Maryland," Jake, who was a sheriff's deputy as well as a Search and Rescue volunteer, said. "None of the other campers seem to know her. We found her under a tree just outside of a rental van. She was probably trying to get away when the tree caught and pinned her." He folded back the blanket covering her. "You can see she was hit pretty hard in the back of the head."

Zach started to look away, but something about the woman's thick brown hair and high white forehead made him look again. He shuddered and went cold all over. "Cammie!"

He didn't realize he'd said the name out loud until the sheriff put a hand on his shoulder. "Do you know her?" Travis asked.

Zach took a step closer and stood over the body. This couldn't be real. He put out a hand as if to touch her, but Travis grabbed his arm and held it. "Zach," he said, his voice firm. "Zach, do you know this woman?"

Zach sucked in a breath, trying to pull himself together. He nodded, then said, "Yes," though the word came out as more of a croak. He was vaguely aware of the other team members gathered around, staring at him.

"How do you know her?" Travis asked.

Instead of answering the sheriff, Zach looked at Jake. "Could I see her arm?" he asked. "Her left arm."

Jake glanced at Travis, who nodded. Jake bent and peeled back the blanket enough to untuck the dead woman's arm. She was wearing a long-sleeved fleece top, blue with white trim. Zach swallowed hard. "Is there a tattoo?" he asked. "Just above her left wrist?"

Jake pushed up the sleeve, and suddenly Zach couldn't breathe. He stared at the blue-and-green butterfly tat, no larger than a dollar coin, the name Laney in script beneath it. He closed his eyes, and Travis gripped his shoulder, steadying him. "Do you know her?" Travis asked again.

Jake nodded and opened his eyes. "That's my sister," he said. "That's Camille. Camille Gregory."

"When was the last time you saw your sister?" Travis asked.

Zach choked back a moan. This couldn't be happening. How could it possibly be happening? Travis repeated the question. Zach forced himself to look at the sheriff. "Four years ago," he said. "At her funeral." Then, to make sure Travis understood, "My sister, Camille, died four years ago."

Chapter Two

Zach sat in the gray-walled interview room at the sheriff's department, gaze fixed on the unopened bottle of water in front of him, but all he saw was Camille. Not the pale, dead woman who had lain on that litter, but Camille as she had been in life—smiling, quick-witted, so smart it took his breath away. Losing her had been the worst thing that had ever happened to him. Was it true that she had been alive all this time and he hadn't known it? That she had died again so close to him and he hadn't been aware that she was here?

The door to the interview room opened, and Sheriff Walker and his brother, Sergeant Gage Walker, entered. "How are you holding up?" Gage asked. A little taller than his brother, the more outgoing of the two, Gage rested a comforting hand on Zach's shoulder. "Do you want some coffee or something?"

Zach shook his head. "No thanks." He looked to Travis. "Can you tell me what's going on?"

Travis slid out a chair across from Zach and sat, while Gage leaned against the wall behind him. "Maybe you can help us fill in some gaps," the sheriff said. "You say your sister's name was Camille?"

"That's right. Camille Louise Gregory."

"How old was she?" Travis asked.

"She was two years older than me," Zach said. "She was twenty-six when we buried her."

"The driver's license we found says this woman was thirty," Travis said.

"That's how old Camille would have been now." Zach massaged his forehead, trying to subdue the pain pounding there. "I don't understand any of this. What was she doing at that campground? And you said she was in a van?"

"The driver's license in her purse identified her as Claire Watson," Travis said. "Does that name mean anything to you?"

"No. I've never heard it before."

"You said you last saw your sister four years ago. At her funeral. So you saw her actual body?"

"No. It was a closed casket. The officers…" He swallowed past the knot in his throat. "The officers who found her body, and the funeral home people, said it would be better that way. But they were sure it was Camille. And my parents identified the body."

"How did your sister die?" Gage asked.

"She was murdered."

The brothers exchanged a look he couldn't decipher. "Who murdered her?" Travis asked.

Zach took a deep breath, though it was hard, as if someone sat on his chest. "The case is officially unsolved, but she was probably killed by one of the Chalk brothers or someone they hired." At the sheriff's puzzled look, he added, "They're a family in Houston, where we're from. Wealthy businessmen, but they're crooks.

You can check with the FBI. They have a file on the Chalk family."

"Why would they kill your sister?" Gage asked.

"She had agreed to testify against them. Two of the brothers—Charlie and Christopher—were charged in the murder of a district court judge. Camille was there that night, at the restaurant where it happened. She testified about what she saw, but the brothers were acquitted." He shook his head. That whole ordeal had been a blur, and time hadn't clarified his memory.

"And you think the Chalk brothers were responsible for your sister's death?"

"That's what the FBI told us they suspected, though there was no evidence they could use to convict the brothers of the crime. They said she was gunned down leaving work—another restaurant job. My parents went to identify the body, and we had the funeral—so how did she turn up here, in Colorado, four years later?"

"You're sure this woman is your sister?" Travis asked. "You couldn't have made a mistake?"

"Camille had a tattoo like that—the butterfly with the name Laney. What are the odds that another woman would have that same tattoo in the same location?"

"Who was Laney?" Gage asked.

"Our sister. Camille's twin. She died when the girls were eleven. Meningitis."

Both brothers were still looking at him like they didn't believe him. "Check with the FBI," Zach said. "I'm sure every bit of this is in Camille's file."

"Does the name Carla Drinkwater mean anything to you?" Travis asked.

"No. Who is she?"

"The van this woman was driving was rented under the name Carla Drinkwater. She had a second driver's license in that name."

He felt dizzy again, like he was falling. He grabbed the bottle of water, twisted off the lid and drank. When he set the bottle down again, his head was a little clearer. "How did she die?" he asked. "I heard something about a tree falling on the van."

"We were waiting to hear back from the medical examiner's preliminary exam," Travis said. "Apparently this woman—Carla or Claire or Camille—was stabbed in the chest. She had been dead several hours by the time that tree fell. I've got deputies out talking to as many of the campers who were in that area as we can find, to try to determine if any of them saw anyone else near her campsite."

"None of this makes sense," Zach said. "You're telling me my sister was murdered—twice?"

"We're still not certain this woman was your sister," Travis said. "How could she be, if your sister died four years ago?"

"I don't know the answer to that," Zach said. "But I'm sure this was Camille. I know my own sister. Can't you get dental records? Or DNA? You can compare it to my DNA. Or my parents—" He stopped. "Have you contacted my parents?"

"Where are your parents?" Gage asked.

"They live in Junction. They came here not long after Camille…after we thought we had buried her. To make a fresh start."

"But you've only been here a few months," Travis said. They must have checked out his background. Or maybe one of his fellow SAR volunteers had mentioned he was new to the group. "Nine months. I moved around a little before I came here to be closer to my parents." He should have stayed with them all along, but he had been so torn up about Camille. It had been a long time before he had been able to think straight and realize he had a duty to look after his parents. He was all they had left. "You need to let me break this to them," he said. "But not until we figure out what's going on."

"Until we have a positive identification, we don't see the need to involve anyone else," Travis said.

"Good." Zach nodded. "They've been through enough." Losing Laney had crushed them. Losing Camille fifteen years later had almost destroyed them.

"Is there anything else you can tell us about your sister that might help us identify her or her killer?" Travis asked. "Do you have any idea why she was in Eagle Mountain?"

"I don't know," he said. "Unless she was here to see me." He swallowed again, fighting a surge of emotion. "Camille and I were close. Especially after Laney died." After her funeral, he had struggled to accept that she was gone from his life.

He had told himself at the time he was indulging in wishful thinking. But apparently, he hadn't been entirely wrong. Camille hadn't been dead then. So was she really gone now?

SPECIAL AGENT SHELBY DRYDEN's first thought upon meeting Camille's brother at his home in Eagle Mountain was that the photograph in Zachary Gregory's file did not do him justice. She knew all the particulars by heart—six foot four, broad shoulders, dark hair, dark eyes. But the file—and the grainy photo that accompanied it—hadn't conveyed the man's brooding nature, the sensual quality of his lips or the heavy-lidded gaze that lent a seductive air to his expression, though she was certain that was not what he had in mind. If anything, Zach Gregory looked thoroughly upset with her. And she couldn't really blame him. Five minutes ago, he hadn't known she existed.

Rather than prolong the inevitable, as soon as he opened his door and she introduced herself and showed him her credentials, she had announced that the woman found dead in that Forest Service campground that morning was indeed his sister, Camille Gregory, aka Claire Watson, that she had been in the Witness Security Program for the past four years and that she had disappeared from her home in Maryland five days ago.

"I understand why you're angry, Mr. Gregory," she said, keeping her voice low in case any of the neighbors in the townhomes around them were eavesdropping. She had driven to Zach's home immediately after confirming Camille's death with the local sheriff's department. She had taken the first flight available from Houston to Junction after the sheriff's department had contacted the FBI with news of Camille's death. Apparently, Zach had been on the scene when Camille's body had been found—not at all what Shelby or anyone else involved would have wanted. Now it was up to her to try to calm him down and find out how much he knew. "As terrible as this was for you and your family, we had to make you believe Camille had died. It was for your own protection. And for hers."

"You didn't do a very good job of protecting her if she's dead now," he said. "If she's really dead this time."

"Yes, she's really dead this time." Shelby glanced to either side. "Could I please come in and talk about this?"

He stepped aside, and she moved past him into the townhome's front room, aware of his bulk looming over her. Camille had referred to her brother as a gentle bear of a man, but Shelby sensed none of that gentleness now. She was used to people being angry with her, but they were usually people who had broken the law or failed to cooperate in an investigation. Zach Gregory was the first she had encountered whose anger she understood. In his shoes, she might have wanted to break someone in half.

He closed the door and turned to face her again. "Let me see your ID again."

She held up her Bureau-issued identification. He peered at it, then at her, and she felt his gaze to her core. Weighing her. Judging whether or not he could trust her. "Shelby Dryden. I don't remember you from the trial."

"If you mean the Chalk brothers trial, I wasn't there." She tucked the ID back into her pocket. "I met your sister after she went into witness security."

"They told us she had been murdered, gunned down by an unknown shooter on her way home from work. They said she had refused a security detail, and that they had no suspects in her death. They said they were very sorry." His mouth was grim, but his eyes had the bottomless look of someone who was beyond exhaustion.

She wanted to take his hand. To try to comfort him. But there wasn't any way to make this whole ugly mess better. Instead, she looked toward the sofa and chairs arranged in front of a fireplace on one side of the large, open living room. "Let's sit down," she said. "And I'll try to answer all your questions."

He followed her and dropped onto the sofa, while she sat on the edge of a low-backed, upholstered armchair on his left. All the furniture looked new, which fit with the information she had, that he had lived in Eagle Mountain less than a year. His home was neat, but as impersonal as a hotel, with no photographs or art on the walls, no books or magazines on the coffee or end tables. The only sign that anyone really lived here was a half glass of water and a half-eaten sandwich on a paper napkin on the table beside the sofa. She must have interrupted him eating dinner.

"Tell me what's going on," he said. "The truth, this time."

She nodded and smoothed her palms down her thighs. "Just know that your sister wasn't forced into anything," she said. "Going into witness security was her choice, as was the decision to fake her death and not tell her family. She felt doing anything else would put you all in too much danger, and we had to agree."

"And she went where? To Maryland?"

"Yes. She started a new life there. She had a townhouse in a nice neighborhood and a job as office manager of a small insurance agency. She made friends. She had a good life."

His expression didn't soften. "She didn't have her family."

"No. And I know she missed you all. She talked about you sometimes." She especially talked about Zach. How she worried her death would send her little brother off course. Camille had blamed herself for putting him in danger, though Shelby had tried to convince her this wasn't the case.

"So what happened?" Zach asked. "Why is she dead now? And why was she even here? Why was she camping?"

"Maybe she thought camping was a good way to hide out. I think she was trying to reach you," Shelby said. "I think she wanted to tell you something. Or warn you about something."

"Warn me about what?"

"I don't know. But looking back on conversations we had before she disappeared, I think she believed the Chalk brothers had learned something that put you in danger. She wanted to warn you to be careful."

"So the Chalk brothers killed her?"

"Probably someone who worked for them, but yes, that's what we believe."

"But you don't have proof." He shook his head. "There's never any proof. Or enough proof. My sister put her life on the line. She sat in that courtroom and told them everything she saw that night at the restaurant. She saw that judge die, and the Chalk brothers were the only ones there, but it wasn't enough to put them behind bars."

"She didn't see the shots fired," Shelby said.

"She heard them!" he protested.

"She couldn't swear there wasn't anyone else there that night. The defense team took advantage of that."

"You know they killed that judge."

She nodded. "Yes. We believe they lured the judge to the restaurant that night. Possibly they offered him money. Instead, they killed him. But knowing isn't enough. We have to have proof."

He leaned forward, elbows on his knees, face buried in his hands. He wore jeans and a blue plaid flannel shirt open over a gray T-shirt. The muscles of his back and arms strained the shirt. He looked like a mountain man. Someone strong and capable, not the baby brother Camille had worried about so much. Shelby waited, giving him time. The house was so silent, not even traffic noises coming from outside.

At last, he raised his head. His eyes were red rimmed, but he looked less angry now. "What are you doing here?" he asked. "Doesn't the US Marshals Service handle witness protection? Or witness security—whatever you call it? Why is the FBI involved?"

"The US Marshals Service is in charge of witness security," she said. "But the FBI is still actively investigating the Chalk brothers. And we will investigate your sister's murder."

"So you drew the short straw and had to talk to me?"

"I volunteered for that." She leaned forward a little more. "Camille was my friend. I know how much you meant to her. Talking to you was something I could do for her."

The grief that flashed across his face was so raw her own eyes stung with tears. He looked away, the skin along his jaw white as he clenched his teeth, his throat convulsing as he swallowed.

She stood and retrieved the glass of water and handed it to him. He took it and drank, then froze and stared at her. "What about my parents? Did you send someone to talk to them, too?" He stood. "I should be there with them. I was waiting until we knew more about what had happened before I talked to them."

"I was planning on talking to them after I visited with you," she said. "We can go together."

He didn't sit back down but rubbed a hand over his face. "Are they safe? Will whoever killed Camille go after them next?"

He wasn't worried about his own safety, only his parents'. That fit with everything Camille had told her. "Junction Police have been alerted to keep an eye on them, but we don't believe they're in any danger." Zach might be a different story, if Camille's suspicions were true. "Sit down and talk to me," Shelby said. "I have some questions I need to ask you, then we'll visit your parents."

He sat, perched on the edge of the sofa, as if prepared to spring up again at any second. "What about my questions? Are you going to tell me what really happened?"

"I'll tell you as much as I can."

He didn't look happy with that answer but pushed on. "You say she disappeared? What do you mean? Was she, like, monitored or something?"

"She had a team with the Marshals Service who kept an eye on her. Not exactly bodyguards, but they watched for anything unusual that might pose a threat, and we— the FBI and the Marshals—tried to stay alert to any developments with the Chalk brothers that might indicate they had located her. And she and I talked every few days."

"Because you were her friend?"

"Yes. And because I'm still involved in the case. She would share anything she remembered about the Chalk brothers in general and that night at the restaurant in particular."

He stilled, as if suddenly transformed into a statue. "Zach?" she asked.

He shook his head, as if to clear it. "Did she tell you anything new?" he asked.

"Nothing big. But sometimes she would remember little details that hadn't come out at the trial. Like she had seen the brothers in the restaurant two weeks before the judge's murder, with a third man. We haven't been able to identify that man, but we're working on it. I stopped by her townhouse four days ago to show her some photographs, to see if she recognized anyone in them, and realized she was gone."

"How did you know she was gone?"

"She had a cat. A gray tabby she named Peter. She had given it to her boss's daughter at the insurance agency. She told the girl she couldn't keep it anymore." Sadness threatened to overwhelm her, and she looked away.

"Camille always loved cats," he said.

Shelby nodded. "I knew if she had given Peter away, that meant she didn't think she would be coming back."

"Where did you think she had gone?"

"I thought at first she had decided to strike out on her own. It happens. People get tired of being watched and protected. Or they believe they'll be safer. They move somewhere else—overseas, out West, to Alaska. They take a new name and start a new life. Most of them know a lot about how to do that because they've been in the program. Some of them are even successful. Some of them return to the program after a while."

"And some of them die," he said.

"Yes. People enter witness security because their life

is in danger. If that threat hasn't gone away, they are always vulnerable to being discovered and eliminated."

"And you think that's what happened to Camille? She was...eliminated?"

"We're still piecing together exactly what happened, but people who get in the Chalk brothers' way usually end up dead."

"And no one is stopping them."

"We're trying," she said. "That's why I'm here now."

"Showing up after Camille is dead doesn't really help anything."

The words hurt. He probably meant them, too. But she was good at hiding her feelings. It was practically a requirement in the Bureau. No one wanted the reputation of being too soft—especially not a woman. "I already told you, I believe Camille was near Eagle Mountain because she wanted to see you," she said. "She was worried you were in danger."

"So she came here to warn me. But why would I be in danger?"

She met his gaze. "I don't know. She wouldn't tell me. I was hoping you had some idea. Do you know something that would upset the Chalk brothers? Maybe something you haven't mentioned before."

"No. And it's been four years since their trial. Why come after me now?"

"If the Chalk brothers thought you knew something about the judge's murder that hasn't come out yet, they might go after you. Maybe something Camille told you that she forgot."

"The Chalk brothers were already acquitted of that

murder," he said. "It wouldn't matter if there was new evidence or not, would it?"

"Only if the evidence implicated someone else," she said.

"Then the Chalk brothers ought to be giving the person who could provide that evidence a medal, not trying to kill them. Their whole case was built on the idea that some mysterious third person stepped out of nowhere to kill the judge and they were innocent bystanders." His face twisted in disgust.

"So you're positive your sister never contacted you. Maybe on social media? She might have used a false name—Claire or Carla, or even Gladys."

"Gladys?" That surprised a harsh laugh from him.

Shelby forced herself not to squirm. "She had a couple of social media accounts under that name. She never posted, but she read other people's posts. Maybe she read yours."

"I don't do social media," he said.

"Never?"

He met her gaze again, his expression hard. "Having the FBI questioning me about every aspect of my life for the year before the Chalk brothers trial made me value my privacy." He stood and stared down at her.

She rose also, though she still felt small beside him. "I'm probably going to have more questions," she said. "I need you to answer them to help me find whoever killed Camille."

"It doesn't matter if you find them if you don't have the right proof," he said. "That's what it came down to with the Chalk brothers before, isn't it? We all know they murdered that judge, but they got away with it. And they probably killed Camille, too. Do you really think you're going to make any difference this time?"

"I'm going to try."

He shook his head. "Go for it, then. Just don't expect me to be any help." He scooped up his keys from the table by the door. "I'm going to see my parents now. You don't have to come."

"I can answer questions for them that you can't." She followed him out the door. "And I'm required to be the one to officially notify them."

"Suit yourself."

She followed him to his truck. When he unlocked it, she opened the passenger door and slid inside. He frowned at her. "You can follow me in your vehicle," he said.

"It's better this way." She fastened her seat belt. She had made the trip from Junction once today. The hour-long drive would give her time to study him and get to know him better.

She felt sorry for Zach, losing his sister not once but twice. But she couldn't let pity get in the way of doing her job. And she was convinced he was lying to her about something. He wasn't going to get rid of her until she found out the truth.

Chapter Three

Zach tried to focus on the dark highway and the terrible task ahead of him—informing his parents that everything they thought they knew about Camille's death was wrong, but that she was more lost to them now than ever. But the woman beside him drew his attention away from these thoughts. He couldn't see her well in the darkness, but every nerve tingled with awareness of her—the vanilla-and-flowers scent of her perfume or lotion, subtle and sexy. Though why anything about an FBI agent should be sexy to him, he couldn't fathom. The agents who had dogged his family every waking hour after Camille agreed to testify against the Chalk brothers had been nothing but annoying.

None of them had been women. None of them had spoken to the family with Shelby Dryden's warmth or compassion. As much as he wanted to resent her for her part in keeping Camille's existence from him, he had a hard time holding on to his anger. Shelby had known Camille in her new life. She said she had been Camille's friend.

He believed that. He could see similarities between Agent Dryden and his sister. Not physical similarities, but they both had the ability to connect with others. Camille had been a great restaurant server, always pulling in big tips because she had a talent for zeroing in on the best way to put a customer at ease. People would confide all kinds of personal secrets to her, then thank her for listening to them. They seemed to sense that Camille truly did care about the lives of everyone she met.

He felt that in Shelby Dryden, too. When she said she was sorry for his loss, the words didn't come across as a rote platitude. She really did care. And he thought she mourned Camille's death and maybe even took her murder personally.

"Thanks for agreeing to take me to your parents," she said, breaking the silence between them. "I think it will be easier for them than having some unknown FBI agent show up on their doorstep."

"You didn't really give me much choice. But yeah, it probably is better this way." He turned onto Eagle Mountain's main street and headed toward the highway.

"I need to ask them some of the same questions I asked you—had they heard from Camille at all? Have they seen anyone suspicious hanging around?"

"No to both questions," he said. "They would have told me if they had. They still talk about Camille all the time." Some of those conversations were painful, but they were comforting, too, keeping the memory of his sister alive. "And they would have told me if they were worried about anyone or anything."

"Do you think they would? Parents often try to protect their children from things like that."

"I'm not some little kid. And I'm supposed to protect

them." His knuckles whitened as he gripped the steering wheel with more force.

They turned onto the highway and headed toward more open country. "Tell me about your mom and dad," she said. "I know what our file says, but the file only contains facts—not a lot about their personalities or emotions."

"They're very strong people," he said. Despite losing two children under tragic circumstances, they still remained invested in life, active and involved, with many friends.

"They would have to be, to have gone through what they have."

"My dad is more outgoing, like Camille," Zach said. "He manages a hardware store and knows all the regular customers. He volunteers with the local parks board and is on the library board." Tightness pulled at his chest. "If someone wanted to find him, it would be easy enough to do."

"What about your mother?"

"She's quieter, like me. She works at home, doing accounting for small businesses. She had a really hard time during the trial. When they told us Camille had been shot, she fell apart for a while. She's been better lately, but…"

"But you worry about her," Shelby said.

He glanced at her, then back at the road. "Would you tell me if they were in any danger?"

"They're not in any danger that I'm aware of," she said. "I want to check in with them and find out if they've noticed anything we haven't."

"You didn't answer my question."

"I would tell you what I could." She paused, then

added, "I have to balance an individual's desire to know with the big picture of whatever case I'm working on. Some cases require more secrecy than others."

He made a sound of disgust, low in his throat, but said nothing. Silence made a wall between them. She shifted in her seat, the fabric of her suit making a rustling sound. "Camille didn't talk about your parents much," she said after a moment. "I think it was too painful for her to do so. But she talked about you quite a bit."

A long silence. But he couldn't shut her out completely. Not when she was his only connection to Camille. "What did she say?" he asked, finally.

"She mostly talked about good times the two of you had together. She mentioned a trip to Cancun—just the two of you. You took a taxi out to Tulum, and when you had finished sightseeing, you discovered all the taxis were gone and you had to talk your way onto a tour bus headed back to the city center."

"She did the talking," he said. "I pretty much just followed her lead."

"She had a powerful personality," Shelby said. "When someone like that dies, it leaves a big hole."

He cleared his throat. "Do you have any brothers or sisters?" he asked.

"No, I'm an only child. My father is a symphony conductor, and my mother is first chair violin in the same symphony. Our lives revolved around rehearsals and performances."

Her answer surprised him. It didn't seem like the kind of background a law enforcement officer, especially an FBI agent, would have. "Do you play an instrument?" he asked.

"Not a note. To their everlasting dismay, I have a tin ear and can't carry a tune. I'm so unlike either of them that I think sometimes they wondered if I had been switched at birth. They still don't know quite what to make of me."

"My parents don't know what to make of me, either." He ran his hands along the steering wheel, surprised by this urge to confide in her. But he felt compelled to continue. "I kind of fell apart for a while, after Camille's funeral. I moved around, never held a job for long. I know it worried my folks."

"But you're here with them now."

"I'm trying," he said. "But I'm not Camille. I'm not Laney." Those two had been the perfect kids, the shining stars. The sunny, outgoing, smart kids, loved by everyone. He was just himself. Too big and too quiet and awkward.

She made a small noise he interpreted as an expression of sympathy, but when he glanced over at her, he saw she was sitting up straight, staring into the side mirror. "What's wrong?" he asked.

"That white Toyota behind us. I'm sure I saw the same vehicle in Eagle Mountain." She leaned toward the mirror, squinting. "I think it's following us."

Her words were so startling and unexpected Zach couldn't make sense of them at first. He glanced in the rearview mirror. There were headlights in the distance, but there was nothing unusual about that. "How can you tell anything in the dark?" This wasn't like the city. Once they were away from town, the darkness engulfed them, only a sliver of moon and stars like broken glass scattered overhead.

"I've been watching it for a while now. It slows down when we slow down and speeds up when we speed up. And it's staying just far enough back that I can't see it too clearly. But I got a better look at it when we passed through that lighted crossroads a few miles back. I'm sure it's the same car I saw near your townhouse in Eagle Mountain."

"Just because you saw the car in Eagle Mountain doesn't mean it's following us," he protested. "It's probably just someone headed to Junction to shop or go to the movies," he said. "It's the closest larger town, so people from Eagle Mountain go there all the time."

"It doesn't have a front license plate," she said. "That's very convenient for a vehicle tailing another."

"Maybe it's from out of state," he said. "And there are a lot of white Toyotas around. Are you sure it's the same one?"

"I'm pretty sure. I can't make out the driver very well. Like I said, it's keeping too far back."

"I don't think we're being followed," he said. "It's just someone else going to Junction."

She settled back in the passenger seat, but tension radiated from her. "You're probably right," she said, without the least conviction in her voice.

She was beginning to freak him out, though he didn't want to show it. "I guess you're trained to notice things like that," he said.

"Yes." She glanced over her shoulder, crouching down a little, as if she didn't want the driver of the vehicle behind them to see her.

"What should I do?" he asked.

"Just drive normally."

He tried to relax and do as she asked, though his gaze returned repeatedly to the lights visible in his rearview mirror. She was right—the vehicle wasn't getting any closer, or any farther away.

They reached Junction, and Zach signaled a right turn. The vehicle that had been following them sped past, continuing straight on the highway. "Guess they weren't following us after all," Zach said.

"I guess not," she said. "Though a skilled driver might go up a block and circle back, if they wanted to throw off suspicion."

By the time he reached his parents' house, his neck ached with tension, but he hadn't seen the Toyota—or any other vehicle—since. He parked at the curb in front of his parents' house and checked the time. It was after nine. "I should have called ahead," he said. "But I didn't want to tell them about Camille over the phone."

"We'll tell them together," she said and opened the passenger door.

Zach's parents lived in a blue-and-white ranch house in a neighborhood full of homes mostly dating from the seventies and eighties, judging by the architecture. Zach led the way to the front door, Shelby just behind him. She looked around, her attitude wary. Was she searching for signs of trouble or the person she thought had followed them here?

He rang the bell and had to wait a long minute before he heard the door unlocking. His father peered out. "Zach!" he said, then looked past him to Shelby. "Is everything okay?"

"Can we come in and talk to you and Mom?" he asked.

By way of an answer, his father stepped aside. Zach

moved past him into the living room, Shelby on his heels. Zach's mother looked up from the sofa, where she was reading, dressed in blue-striped pajamas. While Zach's dad had his son's coloring and facial features, on a much smaller frame, his mother was the image of Camille, older and softer. She looked to Shelby. "Hello?" she asked, a question in her voice.

"Mom, Dad, this is Special Agent Shelby Dryden," Zach said.

His mom's expression changed to one of alarm at the words *special agent*. His father moved to sit beside his wife. "What's this about? Has something happened?"

Zach sat across from his mother. Shelby took the chair beside him. Zach had tried to think of how to break this news to his parents, but there was no easy way. "You've heard of the Witness Protection Program, right?" he asked.

"Oh, Zach." His mother covered her mouth with one hand. "What's happened that you have to go into witness protection?"

"Not me, Mom." He sent a desperate look to his dad, then added, "It's Camille. All this time we thought Camille was dead, she was in witness protection. Or witness security, they call it. In Maryland."

"Camille's alive?" The hope in his mother's eyes was like a knife to the gut.

"No, Mom, Camille isn't alive," he said. "Not anymore."

Shelby leaned forward. "I'm very sorry. I know this is beyond horrible, but Camille died this morning. She was in Eagle Mountain, under an assumed name. Someone killed her."

Shelby continued from there, laying out the story

as simply as possible and answering his parents' questions. He watched his mother as the story unfolded. She seemed to get smaller as she absorbed the words, folding in on herself, her face crumpling. He started to go to her, but Shelby got there first. She clasped her hand and led her to the sofa, murmuring to her. Whatever she said must have been the right thing—his mother straightened and filled out again, more herself.

"I can't believe she was alive all this time," her father said after the whole story had come out. "And you say she was happy?"

"Yes," Shelby said. "She had a job she enjoyed, a house she loved, friends and a cat. She missed all of you. But she was happy."

"Why did she leave all of that to come to Eagle Mountain?" Zach's dad asked. "What was so important she jeopardized her safety?"

"We're not sure, but we believe she might have intended to contact Zach." Shelby glanced at him. "Some things she had heard from friends back in Houston—friends who didn't realize she was reading their social media posts—made her believe Zach might be in danger."

"From the Chalk brothers?" his dad asked.

"Yes. Though we haven't found any evidence that any of you are in danger."

"Except that Camille is dead," his dad said.

"Yes," Shelby said. "She may have been the only target, but we can't be sure. Which is one reason we're working with local law enforcement to have extra patrols in this neighborhood. And if either of you see anything suspicious—a person who looks out of place or anything threatening—you should call 911 immediately."

His mom nodded, her face pinched. "I haven't noticed anything," she said.

Zach squeezed her hand. "There's probably nothing to worry about," he said. "Everybody is just being extra careful." He didn't mention the possibility that they had been followed tonight. Shelby didn't either.

It was after ten thirty when Zach finally stood. His parents looked tired, and he was going to need to stop for coffee if he had any hope of staying awake for the drive home. "If you have any questions, or if you see anything suspicious, call me," Shelby said, and handed them a business card. "I'll be in the area a few more days, and I'm happy to stop by anytime."

"Thank you." Zach's mom embraced her. "It's so much to take in, but it was good to meet someone who knew Camille."

"She was my friend," Shelby said. "And I'm going to do my best to find out who killed her."

Neither of them said anything else until they were in Zach's truck again. "I need coffee," he said.

"Yeah," she agreed, sounding as drained as he was.

Zach found an open coffee shop on the route they had taken in to town, and they placed an order in the drive-through. Then they headed back out of town. "Thanks for coming with me," he said after a while. "That would have been a lot harder without you there."

"I'm glad I could help." That wasn't the first time she had had to notify someone that their loved one was dead, but it was the only time the people in question had to hear the news twice, four years apart. "Your parents are wonderful people," she said. "I would completely understand if they were bitter, but they weren't at all."

"Yeah. I don't know how they manage to stay so strong."

"I told your mom that Camille was one of the bravest, strongest people I knew and that she always said she got those strengths from her parents." She sank back in the seat and sipped her coffee, telling herself she needed to relax. The worst of this day was over. But a flash in the side mirror distracted her, and she glanced over, then sat up straight.

"What is it?" Zach asked, his voice sharp.

Her stomach tightened. Maybe she was wrong, but she didn't think so. "That Toyota is back," she said.

Zach started to turn his head. "Don't look back," she said. "Don't let them know we've spotted them."

He checked his mirrors. "Even if that is the same car, it doesn't mean they're following us," he said.

"No." She forced herself to settle back against the seat. To look relaxed, even if she was anything but. "Don't signal, but make a sharp right up ahead, then another right to go back one block."

He did as she asked, braking at the last moment and swinging hard into the turn. She heard the squeal of tires as the Toyota followed. "Can you tell who's driving?" he asked.

"No. I still can't see anything. Take the next left."

He turned the corner, which led to a neighborhood of narrow, curving streets. He headed up a hill and pulled into the parking lot of a church. "What are you doing?" she asked, alarmed.

"If they're following us, I'm going to confront them."

She grabbed his arm. "That is a very bad idea." She unfastened her seat belt and drew her weapon. Whoever was in that car might spray them with bullets before she had a chance to return fire, but she wasn't going to confront them unarmed.

Chapter Four

They waited in the church parking lot for fifteen minutes, but there was no sign of the Toyota. Was the vehicle parked somewhere on the street, waiting for them to exit? "Should we call 911 or something?" Zach asked.

"We could," she said. And then what? Would the local cops even believe they were being followed? She wasn't sure Zach believed it. "Pull out and see if anyone follows," she said.

Zach blew out a breath. "I feel ridiculous," he said. He started the engine and pulled out of the lot onto the street. No one followed. There was little traffic on the highway, and the vehicles she did see behaved normally, passing them or turning off or receding into the distance.

Neither of them spoke. Was Zach annoyed with her? No, he was probably simply processing his grief and the terrible way this day had turned out.

He parked in front of his townhouse, but didn't get out right away. She waited, sure he would eventually say whatever was on his mind. "Do you really think someone was following us tonight?" he asked.

"I do."

He turned to look at her. The parking lot security light cast a harsh glow across one side of his face, turning it into a macabre mask, all dark, hollowed eyes and downturned mouth. "Why?"

"You may be the only one who can answer that," she said. "What do you know that the Chalk brothers would kill to keep quiet?"

"Nothing!"

The word rang loud in the nighttime stillness. Was he telling the truth? "Maybe it's something you've forgotten about," she said, her voice softer. "Or something you don't think is important. Whatever it is, you need to tell me, so that I can help you."

He shook his head. "I don't think anyone can help me. Camille is dead." He blew out a breath. "And the worst thing is, she died for nothing. All she wanted was to make a difference. To bring the Chalk brothers to justice. But that didn't happen. She's dead, and they're still walking free."

"She didn't die for nothing," Shelby said.

He looked at her, the trick of light exaggerating the dark hollowness of his eyes. But she felt that same hollowness in her chest. Like him, she wanted the sacrifice Camille had made to matter. But that depended on her now. She needed to prove Camille hadn't died in vain. But she didn't know if she was up to the task.

She opened the truck door and slid out. "Good night, Zach," she said. "I'll talk to you tomorrow."

He didn't answer. She walked to her rental car and got in, but she waited until he climbed out of his truck and went inside his townhouse before she started the engine and left the lot. No sign of a white Toyota. No sign of any threat to him, but she couldn't shake the feeling one was there.

INSIDE THE TOWNHOUSE, Zach lay back on the sofa and closed his eyes, battered by warring emotions. After four years, he had thought he was mostly done grieving for his sister, only to learn she had been alive all that time, only to be snatched away from him again when she had been almost in reach. The cruelty of that reality burned in his chest, along with anger that he and his parents, and all of Camille's friends, had been duped.

Yet he knew Camille wasn't cruel. If anything, she was too compassionate, going out of her way to make other people comfortable, even at her own expense. At her funeral, those who had attended had spoken over and over about how generous and considerate she was. Knowing this, Zach could believe she would do anything to protect her family, even if it meant letting them think she was dead and never seeing them again.

And then she had come back here. Maybe she had only wanted to check on him, to make sure he was okay, but he didn't think so. Agent Dryden had been right when she said Camille had come to warn him.

The idea made him sick with guilt, and he forced his mind to think about something else. Agent Shelby Dryden. She was pretty—not beautiful, but with a rounded face and full cheeks and blue eyes that looked right into him, as if she was searching for all his secrets. She looked younger than she probably was. She looked delicate and gentle, but didn't back down from a difficult task. She had to be tough to face down the kind of criminals the FBI investigated, not to mention her fellow agents, who, from what Zach had experienced, were a hard bunch.

So Agent Dryden could be hard, too. But she had also

been gentle with his parents. She had told them everything they wanted to hear about Camille—all the good things to make them believe she had been happy. But how could she have been happy without her family, when they had always meant so much to her?

Zach thought of the car Shelby Dryden had said was following them tonight. A white Toyota. He didn't know anyone with a white Toyota, but there must be hundreds of them in the county. And it seemed odd that someone would follow his truck but never do anything. They hadn't tried to run him off the road or fire any shots or anything.

The idea that someone had been following him, that the Chalk brothers might want to kill him, ought to terrify him. But he didn't feel fear. All he felt was numb. That was pretty much all he had felt for the past four years. Call it a coping mechanism or the aftereffects of grief. Zach couldn't seem to feel the things he told himself he ought to feel.

Five years ago

"GOOD NIGHT, BENNIE! Have a great time this weekend, Amy! Thanks for everything, Oliver!" Camille waved to the last of the night shift at Britannia Pub as they left the restaurant. Parked across the street, Zach watched the trio of friends pass in and out of the glow of the security lights as they walked to their vehicles at the back of the parking lot. Camille turned the keys in the trio of locks on the back door to the restaurant, then slipped the key ring into her purse and headed down the sidewalk, toward the bus stop.

He started the truck and drove until he was even with Camille. She glanced over and a smile lit her face. "Hey!" He stopped and she pulled open the passenger door. "What are you doing here?"

"I didn't like the idea of you taking the bus while your car is in the shop, so I came to give you a ride home."

"You didn't have to do that," she said, even as she settled into the passenger seat. "But I'm glad you did. Devon says he'll have my car ready Friday. The new ignition module is supposed to be in tomorrow."

"No problem," Zach said. He turned the key in the ignition and checked the mirrors. Unlike during daylight hours, when the downtown Houston streets hummed with pedestrian and vehicle traffic, this time of night—almost three o'clock—he had no trouble pulling into the street. Traffic still eased down the streets, but the cars were spaced farther apart, and the only other people on the sidewalk were a couple of men leaning against the wall outside the Salvation Army mission and a man in a chef's checkered pants and clogs hurrying toward the transit station.

They were scarcely a block away from the restaurant when Camille swore. "What is it?" Zach asked, surprised at the outburst from his normally easygoing sister.

"I left my wallet at the restaurant," she said. "I got it out of my locker on my break to pay Bennie the ten dollars he loaned me to cover lunch the other day, and instead of putting it away afterward I tucked it into the little cubby under the hostess stand." She looked up at him, expression pleading. "I know it's late, but I really need to go back and get it."

"It's okay." He turned left at the next street, went

around the block and coasted back to his previous parking spot across the street. "Do you want me to go with you?" he asked.

"No. I'll just run in and get it. It won't take me a second." She unfastened her seat belt and slid out of the truck, then jogged across the street. She stood for a moment opening the locks, then disappeared inside.

Zach rested his wrists on top of the steering wheel and looked toward the corner of the restaurant, which was also the corner of the street. Britannia's front entrance opened onto the cross street, and the red neon of its sign on the side of the building cast a reflection onto the street. The traffic light turned green. By the time it turned red again, he was wondering what was taking Camille so long. He looked toward the alley and the back door of the restaurant, but all was still. He jumped as a loud report echoed down the empty street. Like a car backfiring or firecrackers, maybe over on the next block.

Or a gunshot? Downtown was pretty safe these days, but there was always crime in a city this size. He glanced back toward the corner, and a man ran into the intersection. The solitary figure froze for a moment, lit by the streetlight—a young man in dark pants and a white shirt, his face very pale. He had a prominent nose and chin, his eyes dark hollows in the bright light, his expression one of terror. The young man turned toward him, and instinct sent Zach diving under the dash.

Then the door of the truck wrenched open, and Camille shoved inside. "Go!" she shouted. "We have to get out of here."

Zach straightened. The man in the intersection was gone, and the light was green again. He put the truck in gear and lurched into the street. He drove wildly, in the middle of the street, running at least one red light, but there was no one around to see him do it.

"There! Turn right there!" Camille pointed and Zach wrenched the steering wheel to the right. He sped past a line of parked cars, then slammed on his brakes as he met a concrete barrier. "It's okay." Camille put a hand on his arm. "We'll be okay now. This is a police station."

Zach blinked. Now he saw that the line of cars he had passed were Houston Police cruisers. He looked up and saw the lit sign Police. "What happened?" he asked.

Camille was pale, but she looked so much calmer than he felt. "Someone was in the restaurant when I went inside," she said. "They must have come in after I left the first time."

"How did they get in?" he asked. "I saw you lock the door."

"They must have come in the front door," she said. "They had a key."

"What do you mean they had a key?"

She wet her lips. "If I tell you, you can't say anything to anyone," she said. "Not even the police. Especially not the police. Whatever they ask you, you weren't there, all right?"

"Why can't I tell the police? Cammie, what is going on?"

She leaned closer and gripped his arm. "Charlie and Christopher Chalk own the Britannia Pub," she said. "You know who the Chalk brothers are, right?"

"Of course." Anyone who lived in Houston and watched the news or read a newspaper knew the Chalk brothers. They owned a lot of real estate. Restaurants and bars, apartment buildings, strip clubs, convenience stores. They were rumored to have connections to the mob or to drug cartels or to illegal gambling and prostitution. Maybe they had spent time in prison. Maybe they had murdered people. How much was truth and how much sensationalism, Zach didn't know or care.

"Christopher and Charlie were in the pub when I got there. With another man. Do you know Judge Hennessey?"

"No. How do you know him?"

"Don't you watch the news?" she asked. "He's the judge who got in trouble for not recusing himself from that money laundering trial that ended last week."

"What money laundering trial? And I don't have time to watch the news. I have a life."

"I was having a drink with Diane last week, and they had the TV on over the bar and I saw the story," she said. "Judge Hennessey was accused of taking a bribe, and word was he was going to confess who had paid him."

"Did the Chalk brothers pay him?" Zach asked.

"I don't know," Camille said. "But one of them killed him."

"What?"

"I had retrieved my wallet from the hostess stand and was getting ready to leave when I heard a gunshot. I turned to look, and there was the judge, lying on the floor bleeding, with Charlie and Christopher standing over him. I ran as fast as I could and got back to you. I don't think they know I was there."

"I heard the shot," Zach said. "I thought it was a car backfiring. And there was a guy…"

"What guy?" She grabbed his arm again. "What are you talking about?"

"Just a guy in the street. He ran from the direction of the restaurant. A guy about my age. Dark hair, dark pants, white shirt. Big nose and chin."

She stared at him, eyes wide. "That doesn't sound like Charlie or Christopher. They're both pretty big guys. Charlie must be at least forty. Christopher is a little younger, but he's fat."

"This guy wasn't fat. But he was terrified."

"Did he see you?"

"I don't think so. When he turned toward me, I ducked down."

She gripped his arm tighter, fingers digging in. "You can't tell anyone about this, Zach."

"Why not?"

"The Chalk brothers are terrible people. If they think you saw anything, they will kill you."

"So you're saying we both just keep this a secret?"

"Not both of us," she said. "I'll tell the police what I saw. They don't even have to know you were there."

"Wait a minute—you're saying I should keep quiet because the Chalk brothers will kill me, but it's okay for you to talk? In what world does that make sense?"

"I was in the building when Judge Hennessey was killed," she said. "I was practically in the same room. All you saw was some guy run down the street. He could have come from anywhere. You would risk your life for nothing. And our parents! It's going to be bad enough for them, having me involved in this mess. If you're in it, too, it could be too much for them. You need to be able to focus on taking care of them."

"Who's going to take care of you?" he asked.

"I'll ask for police protection, and I'll get it. I was an eyewitness to murder, and I can help law enforcement convict criminals they've been after for years." Her color returned as she spoke, and her eyes lit with excitement.

"Camille—" He tried to interrupt her, but she rushed on.

"This will work, Zach. You don't have to get involved." She opened the truck door. "Let me out here and drive straight home. I'll tell the cops I ran here from the restaurant. It's not that far."

"I can't just leave you here."

"You have to, Zach. Now go." She slid out of the truck and slammed the door behind her. Then she took off across the parking lot. Within seconds, she had disappeared into the building.

He sat for a long while, gripping the steering wheel, waiting for Camille to return then thinking he should go inside after her. He thought about the man in the street. Zach had seen him for such a brief moment. Was Camille right? Would he be opening himself up to danger for no reason? It could have been someone walking home after a late night, or a street person, terrified by the sound of gunfire nearby.

He texted Camille half a dozen times, but she never answered. Finally, at four in the morning, he headed home. He woke several hours later to a phone call from Camille. "Turn on the TV!" she said. "It's really happening!"

Still groggy, he turned on the television and scrolled through the channels until he came to footage of two men in suits being led away in handcuffs, flanked by half a dozen police officers. He turned up the sound. "…eyewitness statement led to the arrest of the Chalk brothers for the murder of Judge Andrew Hennessey."

"Where are you now?" Zach asked.

"I'm in a safe house. Trust me—I'm being taken very good care of. And so are you and Mom and Dad. If you see more cops that usual, it's because they've promised to keep an eye on you. Just in case the Chalks decide to go after one of you to get to me."

"Mom and Dad are in danger?"

"No. I don't think so. You're all going to be fine."

"What about you? Can they really keep you safe?"

"Don't worry about me. I'll have to lie low for a few months, until the Chalks are safely behind bars, but it will be so worth it. You can't imagine how I feel right now. I've gone from being a server to a crime-fighting hero. I'm thinking I want to go into law enforcement after this is all over. This could be the best thing that ever happened to me!"

"I should tell the cops what I saw," he said.

"No! Don't you dare. You'll just confuse things and put yourself in danger. Promise me you won't do it, Zach. Promise!"

He rubbed his temples, which throbbed from stress and lack of sleep. "You don't think they need to know?"

"They don't. I've told them everything they need. You look after Mom and Dad and root for me from the sidelines. It's all going to be great. You'll see."

Chapter Five

Shelby sat at a table in a small interview room at the Rayford County Sheriff's Department. Next to her, Sheriff Travis Walker listened to the statement of a witness from the campground where Camille Gregory's body had been found. The sheriff had the most perfect poker face Shelby had ever seen. Tall, dark-haired, looking more like an actor hired to play the part of a county sheriff than an actual law enforcement officer, Sheriff Walker had agreed to let Shelby sit in on the interview. Actually, he had said, "Suit yourself," when she had asked to be present for the interview, and then led the way to the interview room.

Brent Baker shifted in the hard metal chair across from them. He tapped his fingers on the table, tilted his neck back and forth, yawned, then smoothed his hands down his thighs. He reminded her of addicts she had seen, jonesing for a hit, except that Baker looked too healthy to have a drug habit. He wore a tight T-shirt that showed sculpted pecs and abs and moved like an athlete. "I camped out there for three nights, rode some of the backcountry trails," he said in answer to the sheriff's question about what he was doing at the campground. "I ran into Carla, and we started talking." He frowned and scooted his chair forward a couple of inches. "She introduced herself as Carla, though I heard later her name is really Camille?"

Travis didn't deny or confirm this. "What did the two of you talk about?" he asked.

Brent scratched his cheek. "Oh, you know, just what a pretty day it was and what a nice campground. She said she had rented the van and was traveling around, seeing the country. I asked if she biked, and she said no, but she was hoping to do some hiking while she was in the area." Another frown. "I prefer biking to hiking, but I asked her if she wanted to go hiking with me."

"Why did you do that?" Travis asked. A legitimate question, maybe, though it made Shelby want to wince. Brent the Biker was clearly flirting with Carla/Camille and wanted an excuse to spend more time with her.

"I thought she was hot," he said. "I was hoping maybe we could hook up." He glanced at Shelby. "No disrespect meant, ma'am."

She nodded. "I appreciate your honesty."

"Did Carla say anything about where she had traveled from or where she was headed?" Travis asked.

"No. She just said she'd been traveling around. She asked if I lived in Eagle Mountain. I told her I was from Lake City, but I'd spent plenty of time around here."

"Did she act nervous, or afraid of anyone?" Travis asked.

"No. She was pretty relaxed. Friendly." The chair squeaked as Brent shifted again. "She turned me down on the hike, though. Said she would probably leave the next day. Then we started talking about the weather. It was clouding up and the wind picked up, and I told her

I had seen a forecast that called for rain. She didn't like that much."

"Did you see her talking to anyone else at the campground?" Travis asked. "Other campers or anyone else?"

Brent cracked his knuckles and scuffed one toe on the floor. "That's why I'm here, right? Right when it first started raining, I came out of my tent to throw a cover over my bike. I looked toward Carla's van and saw this guy running down the road, away from her campsite. I mentioned it to the cop who came around interviewing everybody, and he said I needed to come in and talk to you." He spread his hands wide. "And here I am."

"What did the man look like?" Shelby asked before the sheriff could.

"He was about six feet tall. Kind of thin. He was wearing black pants and a black rain shell with the hood up, so I really couldn't see his face."

"How did he run?" Shelby asked.

Both men stared at her, and she forced herself not to squirm. "Did he have an easy lope, like a practiced runner?" she asked. "Did he do a sort of walk-run thing of someone who's hurrying but doesn't like to run? Or did he run like someone in a hurry to get away?"

Brent nodded. "I get you. He ran like a runner. Long strides, kind of fluid."

"But you're sure he came from Carla's campsite?" Travis asked.

Brent squinted and rubbed the back of his neck. "I'm pretty sure. But maybe he was just out for a jog and stopped by her van to tie his shoe. I mean, it was raining, and I just glanced over." He shrugged.

"Had you seen this man at the campground before?"

"I don't think so. But like I said, he had the hood of his jacket pulled up, and he was running away from me."

"Did he have anything in his hands?" Shelby asked.

"Like what?" Brent asked.

"Anything. A knife?"

Brent's eyes widened. "Is that what killed Carla? We all thought it must have been the tree that hit her van, but the article I saw online said she was murdered."

"Did you see anything in the running man's hands?" Shelby pressed.

"No."

"The man ran away, then what happened?" Travis asked.

"I thought I'd go over and talk to Carla again. It was raining a lot harder, and all I had was a tent, and she was in that nice van, so I thought maybe I could talk her into taking pity and letting me in." He smiled in a way Shelby thought might be intended as charming but reminded her too much of the boyish types who hit on her in bars. As if the way into a woman's bed was to make her feel sorry for you. "I was headed over there when a guy drove in and said I should think about packing up and clearing out because there was a flash-flood warning, and if the creek across the road into camp rose, we'd be cut off. Then some other people came over, and we were all debating the issue. Then the first guy said he would go around and warn the other campers, and I went to take down my tent and get everything into my truck."

"Do you know if the first man talked to Carla?" Travis asked.

"I don't know."

"What was the man's name?" Travis asked.

"Sorry, I don't know that either."

"You only saw the running man one time—is that correct?" Travis asked.

Brent nodded. "Just the one time."

"Did you see Carla at all after you saw him?" Shelby asked.

"No. And I never did get around to talking to her again. Then I saw the tree on her van." He grew still, the sudden cessation of movement striking. "I should have gone over and helped her. Maybe if I'd gotten to her soon enough she would still be alive."

"Or maybe not," Travis said.

After a few more questions that established that Brent had no more information to offer, Travis thanked him, and a deputy escorted him out. Travis turned to Shelby. "I read the file you sent over, and I know the basics about why Camille Gregory was in witness security," he said. "Do you think the Chalk brothers found her and had her killed?"

"That is the most likely scenario," she said. "But we can't be sure."

"Maybe some other guy flirted with her, didn't take no for an answer, then stabbed her and ran away," Travis said.

"Maybe," Shelby said. "She wouldn't be the first woman traveling alone who was murdered. But I don't think so. Camille was very aware of her surroundings. She was in good physical condition, and she knew how to protect herself. She had taken self-defense classes, and she knew that as soon as she moved out of our circle of protection, she was a potential target. She wasn't naive."

"And you think she came to Eagle Mountain to see her brother, Zach?"

"She was worried about him," Shelby said.

"Why was she worried?"

"She learned through social media that a man who said he worked for the Chalk brothers came back to the pub six months ago and talked to a woman Camille had worked with. He wanted to know if Zach was with Camille that night. Camille said he wasn't, but she was afraid the Chalk brothers didn't believe that, and they might hurt Zach."

"Did the FBI follow up on this?" Travis asked.

Shelby gave him a look that let him know what she thought of the question. It wasn't as if she didn't know how to do her job. "We looked into it. We found the guy, but he swore he didn't know the Chalk brothers. He said he was a freelance writer, following a theory he had. It turned out to be nothing."

"Maybe he was lying," Travis said.

"Maybe he was." Fear that he was right made her throat tight, so she had to force the words out. "I told Camille what we had learned, and I thought she was calmer, but then she disappeared. She left a note saying she needed to see her parents, but that she would be back soon, and to please not come after her."

"But you did go after her."

"Of course we did. But we went to her parents'. There was no sign she had ever been there."

"What do you know about Zach Gregory?" Travis asked.

"Not a lot. He's two years younger than Camille, but the two of them were close. Her death—or what he thought was her death—hit him hard. He drifted around a lot after her funeral, dropped out of college, took a series of dead-end jobs. Lately, he seems to have turned things around. He started working at Zenith Mine and joined Search and Rescue."

"You kept tabs on him?"

She flushed. "We kept track of all her family, in case any threats to them surfaced. And it made Camille feel better to know they were all right. Despite what some people might think, witness security isn't about depriving people of their liberty or making them miserable. We do what we can to help people adjust."

"If you had a good idea where Camille was headed when she left WITSEC, why didn't you come after her?" Travis asked.

Shelby wanted to snap that she wasn't an idiot, but reminded herself that in his boots, she would have asked the same question. "She misled us. She left things that made it appear she had gone to see her parents. By the time we realized we had been duped and headed here, it was too late." She would never forgive herself for that. No matter what her bosses said about not getting personally involved with witnesses or victims, Shelby and Camille were friends. And Shelby would never stop feeling she had let her friend down.

"Do we need to be worried about these men, the Chalk brothers, causing trouble in Eagle Mountain?" Travis asked.

"I don't know. It depends if Camille was right and her brother had become a target. If they were only after her, you don't have anything to worry about." She hesitated, then added, "I went with Zach to see his parents in Junction last night. I thought a car followed us from Eagle Mountain—a white Toyota. I thought I saw the same car again on the way home, but they turned off and there was never any trouble, so maybe I was wrong. It wouldn't hurt to keep an eye on Zach for a few days, at least."

If he was displeased to hear this, his expression didn't show it. "What are your plans?" he asked.

"The FBI is conducting its own investigation into the murder. I appreciate you sharing the information you've already uncovered. I'll need to talk to more people who might have come into contact with Camille or her murderer. And I'll stay in town long enough to determine if Zach Gregory is in real danger. If he is a target, we'll do our best to protect him." She owed Camille at least that much.

"HEY, ZACH. I'm really sorry about your sister."

Zach looked up from the ropes he was coiling and saw Sheri Stevens, one of the Search and Rescue veterans who was helping train rookies like him. He hadn't known how to handle these expressions of sympathy the first time Camille died. Four years hadn't made him any better at it. "Thanks," he said and went back to helping to pack the climbing ropes. He braced himself for the onslaught of questions he was sure would come—about his sister, about her murder, about the judge's murder. They had caught him off guard the first time, before and after the trial. Everyone he met back then, from neighbors to news reporters, wanted some scrap of detail from him that would bring the tragedy closer. Why couldn't they understand this wasn't something he wanted to share with anyone?

But Sheri didn't ask any questions, and neither did any of the other members of the team, though several of them asked how he was doing and said they were sorry for his loss. After a while, he began to relax and accept their condolences as sincere.

"Are you up for this?" Danny asked as they prepared to leave for a callout to an ATV accident on one of the Jeep trails.

"I'm good," Zach said.

Danny nodded. "Then let's get after it."

The network of dirt roads that wound through the mountains above town attracted adventurers on dirt bikes and in Jeeps and all manner of four-wheel drive vehicles, but invariably some of them weren't prepared for the steep terrain, tight turns and rough conditions. Zach had already learned that, next to traffic accidents on the highway that led out of town, calls from the Jeep trails were the second most common crises Search and Rescue responded to each summer.

This accident involved a single rental ATV that had rolled on its side. Zach and the others arrived to find half a dozen other drivers and riders gathered around a lanky man with blond hair to his shoulders and a scruffy goatee, who sat on a boulder a few yards from his overturned vehicle. Blood, already drying, trickled from a cut on his forehead, and the right sleeve of his shirt was in tatters where he had evidently scraped it on the rocks. Danny, a nurse, knelt beside the man. "I'm Danny, with Eagle Mountain Search and Rescue," he introduced himself. "What's your name?"

The blond lifted his head to take in the circle of volunteers around him. "Todd," he said. "Todd Arniston. That's *Todd* with two Ds."

"Let's take a look at that head wound, Todd." Danny, who had already donned nitrile gloves, gently probed the cut on the young man's forehead. "This doesn't look too bad," he said and began to clean the wound. "How are you feeling? Any headache? Dizziness?"

While Danny and volunteer Christine Mercer tended to Todd, Zach and some of the others examined the overturned ATV. An older man wearing an All Who Wander Are Not Lost T-shirt joined them. "I saw the whole thing," he said. "I was waiting my turn to navigate this narrow, rocky section of the trail when he came tearing around the corner. He took that curve on two wheels, and he was going too fast to stay in control when he saw the backup of vehicles here. He lost control in the gravel and went over on his side and skid a long way." The man shook his head. "The whole point of being up here in this beautiful country is to take your time and enjoy the scenery—not race around recklessly."

Eldon Ramsey, one of the group's best climbers, circled the ATV. He looked over at Zach. "This doesn't look too banged up, really," he said. "I bet the two of us could get it upright." Eldon, originally from Hawaii, was as tall as Zach and even more muscular.

"Sure," Zach said. "Let's give it a try."

The others stepped back as Zach joined Eldon on the other side of the ATV. "On three," Eldon said. "One… two…three!" They heaved, and with a groan of springs and metal, the ATV bounced onto its tires. Eldon leaned in and set the brake, then slid into the driver's seat and turned the key. The engine coughed, then growled to life. He shut it off and climbed out.

Todd, on his feet now, walked over to them. Danny had cleaned and bandaged the cut on his forehead and the scrape on his forearm. "Thanks." He shook hands with Eldon then Zach. "What are your names?" he asked. "I want to remember you two." He had a pronounced Southern accent, like someone from Georgia or Alabama, Zach thought.

They introduced themselves. "I can't believe there are people who just volunteer to help others way up here like this," Todd said. "I can't thank you all enough."

Danny shouldered his pack and joined them. "It's a good idea to wear a helmet on these rough roads," he said. "Those side-by-sides will tip over easier than most people think."

"And you need to slow down," the older man who had witnessed the accident said. "You could kill yourself or somebody else."

Todd looked sheepish. "I think I've learned my lesson," he said. "I'll take it a lot slower." He moved toward the vehicle. "I'm just glad I can get this down the mountain without having to pay to have someone haul it."

"Are you sure you're up to driving?" Christine asked.

"Y'all said I didn't have any sign of concussion, and I feel fine now." Todd slid into the driver's seat. "I'll take it nice and slow from here on," he said. "I promise." He nodded to Zach and the others. "It was nice to meet you all. Maybe we'll run into each other in town, and I can buy you a beer." He turned the key in the ignition then gave them a thumbs-up. They all moved back as he guided the ATV onto the trail and puttered down the road.

"Should we have let him leave on his own?" Christine asked as they headed back to the Search and Rescue vehicle.

"I can make medical recommendations, but we can't stop him," Danny said. He stowed his pack in the back of the specially outfitted Jeep used by Search and Rescue. "He'll probably be okay. That knock he took on the head wasn't nearly as bad as it might have been. I told him he should check with his doctor to make sure there's no internal damage, but he probably won't."

"If he does run into trouble, there are plenty of people around who can call for help again," Eldon said. He hoisted himself into the driver's seat. "If it was me, I'd have probably driven down. He'll lose his damage deposit on the rental, but that's probably less than the cost of getting someone up here to retrieve the thing."

"That's the first call I've been on with only minor injuries," Zach said.

"We don't get many like that." Danny settled in the passenger seat, and Christine, Zach, Sheri and Caleb piled in the back. "We see a lot of serious injuries on these trails and more than a few fatalities."

"Were you here when that Jeep exploded?" Christine asked. "I still hear people in town talk about that one."

"That was right after I started." Danny looked grim. "The vehicle rolled three times then exploded. There were five people in it, two adults and three children. Two of the children lived, though it was touch-and-go for them for a while." He shook his head. "The organization paid for a counselor to come in and work with us for a while after that one," he said. "I still think of it every time we come up here."

Zach hadn't responded to a fatality yet. Except for Camille, and she hadn't been the victim of an accident or anything. Seeing her lying on that litter had been surreal. He had thought of her as dead for so long that he still hadn't come to terms with the idea that she had lived another life in the past four years, with a different name, a different job and friends he had never met.

"Dealing with the dead is one of the toughest parts of search and rescue work," Danny said. "But we have resources to help. And if you decide you can't handle that part of it, there's no shame in stepping aside. For me, helping the live victims outweighs the sadness from those we couldn't save."

They murmured agreement. Zach didn't think he'd have trouble dealing with dead strangers, but he wouldn't mind if he had to wait until he had more experience with search and rescue work before he found out.

His phone buzzed with a text message as they pulled into Search and Rescue headquarters.

I need to talk to you. When can we meet? Shelby

He frowned. She had signed her name *Shelby*. Not *Special Agent Dryden*. As if the two of them were pals. She had said she and Camille had been friends, but was that true? Shelby Dryden was investigating the Chalk brothers, and Camille had been a witness to a murder where the brothers were present—and probably responsible. The FBI wanted to know everything Camille knew. How could Shelby interrogate his sister and be her friend?

Had Camille told Shelby that Zach was with her that night at the restaurant? Not inside with her, but waiting outside? Had she confided that Zach had seen a man run away from the direction of the restaurant?

Four years ago, Camille had convinced Zach that what he had seen didn't matter. He had managed to believe that right up until the end of the trial, when the Chalk brothers were acquitted of murder. But even then, Camille had pleaded with him not to say anything. "It doesn't make any difference now," she had said. "And if you speak up, they'll kill you. Promise me you'll keep silent. You have to promise me."

So he had promised. He told himself he did it for Camille. So that she wouldn't worry about him. And for his parents, so that they would have at least one child safe and with them. But all this time another thought had festered inside him—the knowledge that as much as he had wanted to protect his sister, he wanted to protect himself more. He was afraid of the Chalk brothers. After Camille had died the first time, supposedly murdered by the Chalks, he had been even more afraid. He had told himself Camille had been right—that his story about the man in the street wouldn't make any difference.

But now Camille had died again—for real this time. Shelby said she had left the safety of her new life to come and talk to him. Someone had found her and killed her. If Zach had found the courage to speak up, would his sister be alive now?

He didn't know how to live with that kind of guilt, but he was going to have to figure it out. He deleted the text message. He didn't want to talk to Agent Dryden. He didn't want to have anything to do with her.

Chapter Six

Eighteen months ago

Shelby tried not to have expectations about the witnesses she interviewed. She wanted to listen to their testimony without any pre-judgment. But she already knew a lot about Camille Gregory—now Claire Watson—before she knocked on the modest bungalow in a quiet Bethesda neighborhood. She had watched the available video of the Chalk brothers trial and Camille Gregory's testimony against them. Camille was the same age as Shelby— twenty-six at the time of the trial—but she had the confidence and composure of someone much older. On the witness stand, she had sat up tall, chin lifted, and spoken clearly, convincingly. She almost looked as if she was enjoying the experience. The prosecution couldn't have asked for a better witness.

But the Chalk brothers had better lawyers, and their own brand of arrogance that had impressed—or perhaps intimidated—the jurors. The chief defense attorney had emphasized over and over that Miss Gregory had not seen either of the brothers shoot Judge Hennessey. She hadn't even seen them holding a gun. She had turned and run before she had seen much of anything at all.

The woman who answered Shelby's knock was smaller than she had looked in those videos—thin, but not fragile. She examined Shelby's credentials and smiled with genuine warmth. "It'll be nice to talk to a woman for a change," she said. "Come on in."

Shelby was prepared for Camille to balk at answering questions she had already been asked over and over in the two and a half years since the night Judge Hennessey was murdered. She knew how to tease out information from reticent witnesses and how to use emotion—anger, sadness, regret—to elicit information they might not have revealed before. She was very good at her job.

But interviewing Camille required none of that. The young woman was open, happy to talk about that night and everything that had followed, as if she hadn't told the same story over and over. What she said matched what was already in her file. She didn't embellish the way so many witnesses did over time, perhaps in an attempt to make their story, or themselves, more interesting. Camille knew she was interesting, the way some people accept that they are beautiful or powerful.

After the first hour, Shelby felt as if she was talking with a girlfriend. Camille had brought out flavored seltzer and popcorn, and they snacked and chatted as if they had known each other for years. Camille really came alive when she talked about her family—her parents, her deceased sister, Laney, and especially her brother, Zach.

"I wish you could meet Zach," she said. "I think you would really like him."

"Is he a lot like you?" Shelby asked.

"He's not like me." Camille tossed a kernel of popcorn into her mouth and tilted her head, considering. "Zach is quieter. More thoughtful. I mean, he really thinks about things before he says anything or makes up his mind. When we were kids, people sometimes thought he was slow, but he's actually really smart. He just takes his time making decisions. Me, I think on my feet. I size things up very quickly. Sometimes, he accused me of being rash, but it was never like that. I just made up my mind fast and stuck to my decision. That night at the restaurant, I knew what I had to do right away."

"Does Zach look like you?" Shelby asked.

Camille ate more popcorn. "We have the same dark hair and eyes, but Zach is taller and just, well, bigger." She held her hands out to her sides. "Not fat, just tall and broad-shouldered and muscular. But to go along with all that brawn, he is almost pretty. Those big, dark eyes and long lashes. I would kill for lashes like that, you know. And he has this mole right at the side of his mouth." She touched her own face to indicate the position. "A perfect beauty mark. When he was little, kids sometimes teased him about it, but then he outgrew most of them and the teasing stopped." She shrugged. "He was always my little brother, no matter how big he got. And I always tried to look out for him."

"You didn't think he could take care of himself?" Shelby asked, fascinated by this picture of the beautiful giant who needed protecting by a woman who was all of five feet six inches tall and weighed maybe 125 pounds.

"Yes and no. Zach was so quiet and easygoing. Too easygoing. I don't think he ever understood how dangerous people could be. How dangerous the Chalk brothers could be." Her expression grew troubled. "When I told him I needed police protection, I think he saw it as me being dramatic." She grinned, showing white, perfect teeth. "Not that I don't occasionally channel my inner drama queen. When it suits me."

Shelby returned to that night at the restaurant, trying to ferret out any detail they might have missed before, but coming up with nothing new. "I know the Chalk brothers can't be tried again for the judge's murder," Camille said. "So what else do you hope to accomplish?"

"I'm reviewing everything in their files, trying to find some detail we've missed that might link them to other crimes," Shelby said.

"I wish I could help you," Camille said. "But I really have told you everything I know."

Shelby gathered her belongings and prepared to leave. "If you think of anything, no matter how trivial, call me," she said and handed Camille her card.

Shelby studied the card, then slipped it into the pocket of her jeans. "Could I call you just to talk? Or go shopping or to lunch or something?"

Shelby blinked. "Uh, sure."

"It's just that I really enjoyed hanging out with you," Camille said. "I think the two of us could be friends. It would be nice to have someone I didn't have to pretend with, you know?"

Shelby nodded. She didn't know, but she could imagine. No matter who else Camille grew close to from now on, there would always be her other, secret life between them. "Call me anytime," she said. "Just to talk or hang out. A person can't have too many friends."

Camille surprised her again at the door by giving her a hug. She felt the other woman's loneliness in that gesture, and a longing that mirrored her own. Being an FBI agent, especially one of the few women in her office, was lonely, too. She and Camille had more in common than Shelby had imagined.

TWO DAYS AFTER arriving in Eagle Mountain, Shelby stood on the doorstep of Zach's townhouse once more, frowning at the smooth black paint of the front door. He hadn't answered her ring, or the knocking that followed. He might not be home—or he might be inside, refusing to talk to her. She had tried his workplace earlier, and a woman there had informed her Zach was out on bereavement leave. She might take her inability to contact him as bad timing, except that he refused to answer her texts or call her back. She understood he was probably still angry about the role the FBI had played in deceiving his family into believing Camille was dead. Frankly, that whole scenario made her uncomfortable, too.

But she hadn't been part of that deception. She hadn't even been with the Bureau back then. All she wanted now was for the two of them to work together to try to figure out who had killed his sister and her friend. She wasn't his enemy.

She walked back to her car, trying to decide what to do next. Before joining the Bureau, she had worked as a sheriff's deputy. The east Texas town she had worked for had been a little larger than Eagle Mountain and not as scenic, but she had investigated her share of crimes. It was one of those crimes—a kidnapping and multiple murder—that had brought her to the attention of the Bureau.

She needed to put herself back into the role of an investigator. Local law enforcement was being as cooperative as any of them ever were when the Bureau swooped in to take over a case on their turf. They had promised to share any information they uncovered about the crime, but that wasn't enough. This was Shelby's case, so she needed to investigate it herself.

She consulted the report she had received from Sheriff Walker, then pulled up a map of the area on her phone, plugged some coordinates into her GPS and began to drive.

Twenty minutes later, she eased her rental car down a rutted, rocky road toward the Piñon Creek campground. The car's springs groaned in protest as she sank into a pothole, and she winced at the screech of metal on rock as she climbed up out of the hole. Mud spattered the sides of the vehicle and spotted the windshield when she splashed through water running over the road—the last remnants of the flood three days ago.

At last, she spotted the sign marking the entrance to the campground and turned in. A kiosk had a list of the rules and a map showing the layout of all the campsites. The sheriff's report said Camille's body had been found in site number 47, near the back of the campground.

She drove slowly along the dirt road. Only half a dozen sites were occupied, and she saw no people at any of them. Were they away for the day, hiking and Jeeping and fishing and whatever else people came here for? Or were they hiding inside their campers and vans, suspicious of the stranger who was clearly not a camper, moving into their midst?

Even if she hadn't noted the number of the site where Camille had been found, she would have known which one it was by the yellow crime-scene tape that still fluttered from the stunted piñon trees. She parked in site 46, across from 47, and walked over.

Tracks in the mud showed where a wrecker had towed the rental van away. The trunk and branches of a mostly dead tree lay next to the tracks, its stump like a broken molar jutting from the red-brown dirt. The other campers, seeing Camille's body on the ground beneath the tree, had assumed it had fallen on her. But Shelby doubted the impact from this half-rotted trunk could have killed her. And, of course, it hadn't. Had her killer pushed the tree over or managed to arrange for it to fall in order to hide his handiwork a little longer and allow him time to escape?

She searched for other tracks in the mud—shoe impressions or tire or bicycle tracks—but the prints of first responders and other campers, and the flood itself, had wiped out anything that was likely to lead to Camille's killer. She paused to study the deep treads of a man's hiking boots, overlaying the van's tracks where it had been pulled from the campsite. Of course, the crime-scene tape would draw other campers to look. Who didn't love a good mystery?

"What are you doing here?"

She whirled to find Zach Gregory stalking toward her. She forced herself not to flinch or step back. He was a big man. Intimidating. And despite all the stories Camille had told her about her smart, funny, kind brother, Shelby didn't really know him. Grief changed people, and not always for the better. For all she knew, Zach Gregory had a violent streak his sister had never seen. "I'm trying to find out everything I can about Camille's death," she said, keeping her voice calm. "Is that why you're here?" She should have thought of that before. Maybe Zach hoped to feel closer to his sister by revisiting the place where she had died.

He came to stand beside her. Uncomfortably close. She caught the scent of pine, perhaps from where he had brushed against the piñon branches, and heard the heaviness of his breathing, as if he was struggling to control his emotions. "I looked around," he said. "I didn't see anything."

"I was wondering about that tree." She nodded toward the broken trunk. "You probably know more about these things than I do. Do you think it just fell, or did the killer push it over or do something to make it fall?"

The question surprised him; she could tell. He glanced at her, then walked over to the trunk. "It looks pretty rotten," he said. He kicked at it, and bark flaked off. He bent closer and she did also, her face close to his. He had a scar by his left eye from where he had fallen on his bicycle when he was eight and had to have stitches. There was something so intimate about knowing that story, especially when he knew nothing of her childhood.

"You can see where it broke." He pointed to the jagged surface of the stump, the wood in the center dry and crumbling. "And it looks like there was a hole here." He pointed to a vacant area just above the roots on one side. "Maybe an animal dug this out to use as a den. That would have weakened the tree on this side."

"So maybe the killer saw that and shoved the tree over?" Heart beating a little faster, she moved over to the trunk. "Where would he have pushed, do you think?"

Zach joined her in examining the trunk. He stepped over it, then rolled it toward her slightly. "The hole I was talking about is right here." He pointed to the broken end of the trunk, the smoothed edge of a hole clearly visible. He stepped back over the trunk to stand beside her, then carefully tipped that side up.

"Is it heavy?" she asked.

"Not very."

He was several inches taller and more muscular than the man Brent Baker had described seeing leaving Camille's camp. "Could a smaller man, one not in as good shape, have pushed it?" she asked.

He straightened, and his gaze burned into her. "You have a suspect?"

"We have a description of a man who was seen leaving Camille's campsite about the time she probably died," she said. "We don't have a name or any definite identification."

"What's the description? Who saw him?"

"One of the other campers saw him. And the description isn't much—about six feet tall, on the thin side. He wore dark clothing and a rain shell with the hood pulled up, so we have no idea of his hair color or what his face looked like. He moved like a runner."

Zach looked back toward the tree. "If the guy was in decent shape, he probably could have pushed over this rotten tree."

Shelby bent to examine the tree trunk once more, estimating where the killer might have put his hands. "If you were doing something like that, how would you do it?" she asked.

"What do you mean?"

"I mean, would you put your hands on the trunk and shove, or find a big branch and whack the trunk?"

"I'd put my shoulder to it and give a big shove," he said. "Get some leg strength into it, as well as upper body strength."

She visually measured the trunk again. "So his shoulder would have been about here." She touched the tip of her fingers to a spot on the trunk.

Zach bent to examine the spot. "Up about six inches, I think."

She brushed her hands up six inches, studying the rough bark. Then she stilled, holding her breath. "Is that a hair?" Zach asked.

The single hair, perhaps six inches long, glinted in the sunlight, then disappeared as she straightened enough to reach into her jacket and pull out her phone. She snapped several photos, hoping they would show the hair in place. Then she tucked the phone away and pulled out her keys. "Go to my car and open the trunk. There's a small duffel bag in there. Inside the duffel is another smaller, black zippered pouch. Bring that to me, please." She kept her hand on the trunk, afraid if she moved, she would never find the hair again.

Zach took the keys and loped away. He was back a few moments later. She unzipped the pouch and took out a plastic evidence pouch. "Hold this." She handed the pouch to Zach, then felt in another pocket of the pouch for a small case, from which she withdrew a pair of tweezers. She used the tweezers to ease the hair from where it was caught in the bark. She carefully inserted the hair into the pouch, then sealed it. She labeled it with the date, time and location where it was collected, then signed across the seal.

"Can I see?" Zach asked.

She held the pouch up to the light so they could both look. The single hair, a light brown or dark blond, glinted in the light. She said a silent prayer of thanks that the hair was not dark, like hers and Zach's. She didn't have to worry that one of them had inadvertently deposited their own hair on the log in the process of examining it.

"Do you think that belongs to the killer?" Zach asked.

"I don't know." She tucked the bag into the pouch and zipped it closed. "It could belong to another camper who stayed here. But if we do find a good suspect for the murder, DNA might help prove he was here in the camp, and that could go a long way toward a conviction, depending on what other evidence we have."

"They had an eyewitness statement for Judge Hennessey's murder," he said. "That wasn't enough to get a conviction."

"We'll need to do better next time."

"Do you think there will be a next time?" he asked. "From what I understand, law enforcement has been after the Chalk brothers for years, and they've yet to make anything stick."

"We're not going to stop trying," she said. "They're going to make a mistake."

"That was one of the hardest things when we thought she died right after the trial," he said. "That she had sacrificed everything to testify against those crooks, and it meant nothing."

"It didn't mean nothing." She gripped his arm, not even realizing she had done so in her desire to make him understand that Camille's sacrifice hadn't been foolish or useless. "We weren't able to put the Chalk brothers behind bars, but we're still investigating them. They have committed other crimes—we're sure of it. And I wish I could make you understand the way testifying at that trial transformed Camille."

"What do you mean?" He didn't look at her as he asked the question, but down at her hand around his arm.

She released her hold on him and took a step back. "I didn't know her before the trial," she said. "But when I spoke to her about it, she spoke with such pride about what she had done. She told me she had spent years feeling guilty that she wasn't doing more with her life. She wanted to make a difference in the world, but she didn't have money or power, and she hadn't excelled in school or in sports. Her life was so ordinary, and then she had decided to speak up about what she saw in the restaurant that night. She had power over Charlie and Christopher Chalk in those moments, and she had the influence to show others that they could speak up, too. Though she was working at an insurance agency as part of her new identity, she was taking college courses, too. She wanted to work as a victim advocate, and she was so excited about everything ahead of her."

"But she threw all that away to come see me."

"I don't think she thought of it that way," Shelby said. "I think she intended to talk to you, then to come back. We had protected her for four years. I believe she trusted us."

"She didn't trust you enough to tell you whatever it was she wanted me to know."

Hearing him say what she had thought so many times hurt more than she had anticipated. "No, she didn't," she said. "But I'm doing what I can now to try to make that up to her." She turned away. "Let's look around a little bit more and see what we can find."

But all they found was a site swept clean of any other evidence. She consulted the sheriff's report again. Deputies had collected half a dozen soggy cigarette butts, a faded and bent beer can, two bottle caps, a gum wrapper and half a plastic water bottle, none of which were likely related to either Camille or her killer.

"Who was this camper who saw this guy with Camille?" Zach asked when they were back at Shelby's car and she was stowing the evidence bag in the trunk.

"I'm not going to tell you his name," she said. "You don't need to talk to him."

He shoved his hands in his pockets. "Maybe he would tell me something he wouldn't tell the cops."

"Or he might feel threatened and accuse you of intimidating a witness." At his thunderous look, she rested a hand on his arm again. "I know you want to do something to help, but there really isn't anything. I promise I'm going to pursue every lead. Camille was my friend, and finding the person who killed her is important to me."

"Were you even going to tell me about this man?"

"I was if you had ever returned my calls or texts."

He flushed and looked away. "I didn't feel like talking to anyone."

"I need you to talk to me," she said. "I especially need you to tell me if you see anything or anyone suspicious. You know this town better than I do. You would recognize someone who was out of place when I might not."

"Lots of tourists visit here, especially in summer," he said.

"Has anyone been paying unusual attention to you?" she asked. "Have you noticed anyone following you or hanging around your townhouse?"

He shook his head. "There isn't anyone. I think that car the other night was just a coincidence, not someone following us."

Maybe. But maybe not. "I need you to help me," she said.

"With what? You just said there isn't anything I can do."

"Maybe I was wrong." She considered him. Hurt etched every line of his face and every angle of his body. He looked so vulnerable, despite his powerful physique. "Tell me, why do you think Camille came here, to this campground? I mean, why do that instead of going straight to you? Eagle Mountain is a small town. If she knew you were here, she wouldn't have much trouble finding you."

He frowned, but she could see he was seriously considering the question. "Maybe she wanted to make sure no one was watching her," he said. "No one she might inadvertently lead to me."

"So she was cautious like that?"

He shook his head. "Not cautious. She was always pretty daring. But not rash. She made quick decisions, but they were almost always the right ones. She was smart. It was true she didn't do that well in school, but that was because classes bored her. She always wanted to be active. Like you said, she wanted to make a difference."

"Most people aren't like that," Shelby said. "Most people wouldn't risk so much to tell the truth."

"I think it had a lot to do with Laney dying," he said. "When she got that tattoo, she told me it was to remind her that she was living for two people now."

"That helps me," she said. "Knowing what motivated her. Can I come talk to you again about her?"

"Yeah. Sure." His eyes met hers, and the depth of that gaze, the openness, made her unsteady. "It would help me, too," he said. "Talking about her, to someone else who knew her."

"Then it's a deal." She got into her car before she did something wildly inappropriate like throw her arms around him. He looked like he needed a hug, but she probably wasn't the right person to give it. She was already in trouble with her supervisors for getting too personally involved with witnesses in her cases. She was well aware that they hadn't sent her to Eagle Mountain because they expected actual results. They thought exiling her to this remote mountain town for a week or two might teach her a lesson about what it took to get ahead in the Bureau. They didn't seem to understand that for her, getting ahead wasn't nearly as important as getting the job right.

Chapter Seven

Four and a half years ago

Zach stood at the window of his childhood bedroom and peered through the blinds at the reporters lined up on the sidewalk in front of his parents' house. News vans, white satellite dishes angled toward the sky, crowded curbs and blocked the neighbors' driveways. Ever since someone had leaked Camille's name to the media as the key witness in the upcoming Chalk brothers trial, it had been like this. Zach and his parents had to run a gauntlet every time they left the house.

Zach had moved back home shortly after Camille had been relocated to a safe house to await the trial. At first, it hadn't been so bad. His parents were shaken, but they were strong people, and they were proud of their daughter for taking this stand.

But then the media attention had focused on them. Unwilling to allow his parents to face the constant presence of the reporters alone, Zach had asked for leave from his job. When that had been refused, he had resigned. At least he was big enough to intimidate all but the most forward reporters when he went out to buy groceries or run other errands.

A flash winked—someone taking yet another picture of their house. He stepped back from the window, and his cell phone vibrated. He didn't recognize the number. This was probably a reporter, too, so he silenced the call. Seconds later, his voicemail alert chirped. Bracing himself for yet another appeal to "just answer a few questions" he called into his mailbox.

"Zach, it's me! I have a new number." Camille's excitement carried through the phone. He pictured her pacing, the way she often did when she was on a call, as if she had too much energy to remain still. "Top secret and super secure and all that. Call me."

He hit the call back button, and she answered right away. "What do you think you're doing, ignoring me, you goof?" she demanded.

"I thought you were a reporter," he said. "Those are the only calls I get these days. That, and the occasional stranger who wants to share his conspiracy theory related to the Chalk brothers."

"I'm sorry about that. The feds are still trying to figure out who leaked my name to the press. But I don't think it matters, really. I mean, my name was bound to get out there when I testify at the trial next week."

"How are you doing?" he asked. *Where are you? When can I see you?* But he had learned not to ask those questions since that information, too, was top-secret. He accepted this was for her protection, but he hated not being able to see her. This was the longest they had been apart in their lives. Even when they had each gone away to college, they had come home for holidays and had visited each other's schools.

"I'm great," she said. "Everyone has been so nice, and

this place where I'm staying is super posh. Some rich guy must be lending it to the government. Anything I want, they're bending over backward to give me. I feel like some pampered celebrity. I guess the cops have worked so long to try to get something on the Chalk brothers, and I'm giving it to them, so they can't do enough for me."

"Are you nervous about the trial?" He certainly was.

"No. I've been working with the prosecution on my testimony. They want to prepare me so the defense team doesn't rattle me. I feel really prepared, and I'm excited, really."

"Why is that?" Why be excited about facing a couple of murderers who probably wanted her dead? His stomach turned at the thought.

"I feel so strong!" Camille said. "Ever since Laney died, I've been trying to figure out what I should do with my life. I mean, we were identical twins. Exactly alike, except that she got sick and I didn't. Why was I spared, unless it was to do something important? I think this is it."

"I don't know if I believe life works like that," he said.

"I never went back to work after I left for the night before," she said. "Yet that one night—the night Judge Hennessey was murdered—I left my wallet and had to go back. If that hadn't happened—something that had never happened before—I wouldn't have been there and heard that shot and seen the Chalk brothers standing over him. And I wouldn't be here now."

No. She would be home with the rest of them. Safe. "I was there, too," he said.

"Don't say that. You weren't there. You didn't see anything."

He wanted to argue, but he didn't. Presumably, she was talking on a phone supplied to her by the FBI. They might have the phone bugged. Maybe they were listening in right now. "I want to do whatever I can to help," he said.

"You're doing it by staying with Mom and Dad. How are they?"

"Okay. They're really proud of you."

"I'm trying to make them proud. I was talking to a couple of the agents, and I think after the trial I might enroll in the law enforcement academy. Either that or law school. I haven't decided. But I really think I'm meant to help bring bad people to justice."

"When you were thirteen, you thought your destiny was to open an animal sanctuary." She had been raising a litter of abandoned puppies at the time.

"I'm an adult now. And this is serious. I could never do this—give up my job and my friends and you and Mom and Dad—if I didn't believe this was really important."

"I know. But we miss you."

"Once the trial is over and the Chalk brothers are behind bars for good, I'll be able to come home. We'll have a big party or something."

"I feel like a coward, letting you take all the heat." There, he said it. Any feds listening in could make of that what they would.

"You're not a coward," she said. "But I'm the one with the information the prosecutors need. If anything else came up right now, with the trial so close, it would only muddy the waters. Your job is to take care of Mom and Dad. We're still a team—we just have different roles to play."

Camille was the star in this production, and she was

loving it. She would never say so, but she had always had a flair for drama and a desire for attention. Maybe it really was because her twin had been taken from her. She was missing that part of herself, and this was a way to fill that void.

He didn't know. He wasn't a psychologist, and he didn't really care what motivated Camille. He only wanted her safe and home again. If she thought that would happen faster if he kept his mouth shut and his head down, he would do that. No matter how much it hurt to think about. "I love you," he said.

"I love you, too. And don't worry. Everything is going to be fine."

SATURDAY WAS A training day for Search and Rescue volunteers who had been with the organization for less than a year. Veteran volunteers Eldon Ramsey and Ryan Welch taught the class, which focused on climbing skills with an introduction to rigging ropes for various rescue scenarios. "Don't worry about memorizing all of this now," Eldon said. "Just focus on the idea that every situation is unique. Learn the basics, and you'll begin to see how to apply things like anchor points and leverage to the various scenarios you might encounter."

"Being in good shape and building strength will make everything easier for you," Ryan added. "But the right rigging allows us to safely lift an accident victim or another rescuer from a dicey situation without having to rely solely on brute force."

"But being strong doesn't hurt," Eldon said, and nodded at Zach. The two of them were easily the biggest team members.

They practiced working with the various brake bars, pulleys and other equipment for rigging, discussed safety precautions and things to avoid, then left with the assignment to spend at least one evening in the next week at the local climbing park, working on their climbing skills.

Afterward, Zach approached Eldon. "I always thought I was too big to be much of a climber," he said. "All the rock climbers I see are smaller and lighter."

"Not all of us are string beans." Eldon set aside the gear he had been packing away and faced Zach. "A lot of climbing is about using your legs to push you up. When things get really vertical, we have to haul more mass up with our arms and shoulders than the wiry, lighter guys, but we also have more muscle to rely on, so it evens out. I'd say the only real disadvantage is in tight spaces."

Zach nodded. "I guess I just need to get out there and try it."

"We should get together after work one day this week," Eldon said. "I can show you a few tips."

"I'd forgotten that you work for Zenith, too," Zach said.

"You want to head out to Caspar Canyon Wednesday after work?" Eldon asked.

Zach had never been to the popular climbing area, so why not make his first visit with an expert? "Sure. That would be great."

Eldon turned back to the duffel bag of gear. It clanked as he slipped the strap onto his shoulder. "Don't stress too much about the climbing," he said. "It's important to know the basics, but we don't all have to excel in every area. And big guys like us can always contribute."

Zach nodded. His size had always made him stand

out in a crowd, but working search and rescue was the first time he had seen that as an advantage. He left the meeting feeling good about the progress he was making. He was fitting in well with the team, and he was even making a friend in Eldon. He hadn't really had a friend since Camille had disappeared from his life after the Chalk brothers' acquittal. He had told himself he didn't want to be close to anyone, but lately, he'd begun to feel differently.

That afternoon, the morning's discussion of the need to stay in shape still on his mind, he decided to go for a run. He didn't much like running, but at least around here there were trails that offered more scenery than a high-school track. He parked at a local trailhead and set out. He hadn't gone far before he heard someone coming up behind him. He slowed and looked back and was startled to see Shelby Dryden.

Dressed in black leggings and a formfitting black-and-purple Lycra top, a wide headband holding her dark hair back from her face and dark glasses blocking the sun's glare, she didn't look much like an FBI agent. She slowed as she neared him, and grinned. "I didn't know you were a runner, Zach," she said.

"I'm not, really." He turned and began to jog again, the fine grit of the trail crunching beneath his feet. "But I have to stay in shape for search and rescue work. Some of our rescues require hiking, and sometimes running, for miles."

She easily kept pace with him. "I have to pass a physical every year with the Bureau," she said.

"Have you ever had to run down a bad guy?" he asked.

"Not with the Bureau, but once when I was a sheriff's deputy, I chased a shoplifter two blocks and tackled him."

"I'll bet you were a hero for that," he said.

"Not exactly." She grimaced. "I was reprimanded because it made a bad impression for the public to see me tackle someone on the sidewalk."

"How did you end up with the FBI?" he asked.

"There was a case in our town, a multiple murder and a kidnapping. The suspected murderer was wanted on federal charges, so the FBI got involved. They had already given up the woman who was kidnapped for dead, but I kept digging and figured out where she probably was. I was right, and that got the attention of the special agent assigned to the case. He suggested I take a course at Quantico." She shrugged. "The sheriff I was working under wasn't very happy about being shown up by a woman—his words—so I decided maybe there was more opportunity for me with the Bureau."

"How long have you been a federal agent?" he asked.

"Three years. I met your sister not long after I graduated from the Academy. I was just supposed to interview her to update our file on the Chalk brothers, but the two of us really hit it off."

Zach nodded. He was getting winded, making it harder to talk, though Shelby was scarcely breathing hard, despite the higher altitude and steep climb.

"Camille and I used to run together," she said.

"Seriously? She was never one for working out or sports or anything."

"She told me one of her first WITSEC handlers was a runner and she would go out with him. It was something she could do that made her feel safe. That was before she moved to Maryland and was given her new identity. That first six months or so, before people settle into their new lives, is tough on everyone. They don't have jobs or friends, they're cut off from their families and they're not supposed to go anywhere alone. A lot of people can't stick it out, but Camille did."

"She was always stubborn." And independent. She had been determined to testify against the Chalk brothers. Just her, by herself. She would bring them down alone. She had made Zach believe she didn't need his help.

"I have her laptop."

He stumbled, then stopped and stared at her. She stopped also and turned back to him. "The sheriff's department recovered it from the rental van at the campsite."

Camille's laptop. Something personal that she had touched. "What's on it?" he asked.

"I haven't looked at it yet."

"Can I see it?" he asked.

She frowned. "I don't know if that's a good idea."

"There might be things on there—things she's written that you don't understand that I would. I mean, we grew up together. We were close. I know how her mind works." Or he used to. Camille had literally become a different person in the past four years. One he hadn't known.

"Let me see what I find first," she said. "If I think you can help me, I'll let you know."

"I want to see it," he said. "I mean, a laptop. That's personal, you know? If she's written things in files on there or searched particular websites or even downloaded certain games, it would help me know what was going through her head these past few years." He stared at the ground, wishing he was better at expressing himself. "It would make what happened seem more real, I think."

"I can't make promises," she said. "But I'll see what I can do."

It wasn't the answer he wanted, but it was better than he could have expected from most people. Most agents. He had thought from the first that Shelby wasn't like those unemotional, by-the-book agents his family had dealt with before and during the Chalk brothers trial. Maybe it was because Shelby had known Camille. The two of them had been friends. He liked knowing Camille had had a friend in her new life without him.

"Come on," she said. "Let's finish our run."

They set out again, Shelby taking the lead again. Zach didn't mind. She made an attractive picture, pounding up the trail ahead of him. She wore a small black pack—he wondered if it contained a gun. Probably. It must be a strange life, to believe you had to go everywhere armed.

"Did Camille date anyone in Maryland?" he asked.

Shelby slowed her pace a little to drop back and jog beside him. "Why do you want to know?"

"I'm trying to imagine what her life was like. She had a job and I assume an apartment or a house. Did she have a boyfriend? Someone more serious?"

"She had a house. A little bungalow near the park where we jogged. And she dated a few guys. One of the only complaints I ever heard her make was that she felt she couldn't have a real relationship with a man because she could never tell him the truth about the past."

"Do people do that—I mean, do they get married and have kids and stuff and their spouse never knows the truth?"

"I think some of them do. Others choose to tell the truth, and then the spouse has to be sworn to secrecy. But they make it work. Relationships are full of compromises. I guess this is just one more. But you would have to be really certain about the other person before you revealed that you were in witness security. Your life could depend on it."

"It makes me sad, knowing she felt she couldn't really be close to someone."

"She had one serious relationship," Shelby said. "With that first WITSEC handler—the guy she used to jog with. His bosses figured out he was developing feelings for her and reassigned him somewhere across the country."

He stopped again. "Wait a minute. They already took everything else away from her—they took that, too?"

"It's not a good idea for marshals and the people they're supposed to protect to get involved," she said. She pushed her hair back and readjusted the headband. "But yeah, it was pretty awful. But probably for the best."

"Because everybody has to play by the rules?"

"Because if he had really wanted to be with her, he could have found out where she was resettled. He would have had access to that information or known someone within the Marshals Service who did. It might not have been easy to uncover, but if he really loved her, he could have found out. But he didn't. Which tells me that once he was away from her, his feelings cooled."

They started running again. Zach focused on keeping an even pace, on breathing and on the trail. Anything but his sister and what must have been a lonely life so far from the people who loved her most.

They reached the top of the trail and began to run along a ridge. Zach caught his breath and his pace became easier. "What about you?" Shelby asked. "Are you involved with anyone in Eagle Mountain?"

"Isn't the answer to that question already in my file?"

"It isn't," she said. "There's no personal information at all."

"Huh." He looked away. "Then why bother keeping a file?"

"We kept track of your whereabouts in case there was any threat to your safety from the Chalk brothers."

"And is there?"

"Not that we've been able to ascertain."

"But you said Camille came here because she thought I was in danger."

"That was what she thought, but we never found any evidence to prove that. Which is one of the most frustrating things about her disappearance. If she had stayed put, both of you would be safe now."

He heard the anger in her voice—and the grief. "Maybe whatever she was worried about is somewhere on her laptop," he said.

She nodded. "Maybe so."

"Will you tell me if it is?"

She pushed the sunglasses to the top of her head and looked him in the eye. "If you're in danger, I'll tell you," she said. "Even if I'm not supposed to."

She didn't wait for his reaction, but turned and took off down the trail, running hard, putting distance between them.

Chapter Eight

"Do you have any suspects?" Shelby's supervisor, Special Agent in Charge Donald Lester, got straight to the point when he contacted her Monday afternoon. Though she had been sending regular reports of her activities in Eagle Mountain, this was the first time they had spoken since her arrival.

"Not yet," she replied. "I'm hoping we can get DNA results from the hair I submitted—"

"What about the brother?" Lester interrupted.

"Zach?"

"He was in town. Maybe his sister contacted him and arranged to meet. He was upset, felt betrayed—whatever. They argued, and he killed her."

"Zach Gregory was one of the first responders on scene when Camille's body was discovered," Shelby said. "He was genuinely shocked."

"You weren't there," Lester said. "Maybe he's a good actor. He could have killed her, then returned to the scene with Search and Rescue and faked his surprise."

Zach? Kill his sister? "Sir, I don't think—"

"Find out where Zach Gregory was at the time his sister was murdered," Lester said. "Don't rule him out until you have proof."

"Yes, sir." Even though part of her resisted the idea that Zach had anything to do with Camille's death, she saw the sense in ruling him out.

"If Gregory isn't responsible, do you have any reason to believe Camille Gregory's killer is still in the area?" he asked.

"I doubt it, sir," Shelby said. "If this was someone hired by the Chalk brothers, he wouldn't be likely to stick around."

"Then you won't accomplish anything by staying there longer," Lester said. "Focus on the brother, and if you can clear him, I'll reassign you."

She tightened her grip on the phone. "I'm getting closer to discovering what sent Camille to Eagle Mountain in the first place," she said. "She believed her brother was in danger, and if we found out why, that could point us to new charges against the Chalk brothers."

"We know they've committed plenty of crimes," Lester said. "Finding enough proof to put them behind bars has been a problem."

"I'm looking for that proof, sir. I have the laptop recovered from Camille's rental van. I'm hoping it will have something useful on it."

"You can analyze a laptop here in Houston," Lester said.

"Yes, sir. But I want to dig deeper into the brother. He may know something he's not saying."

"Do you think Camille contacted him before she was killed?"

Shelby considered this. "I don't think so. He was truly shocked when I told him about her time in witness security. But Camille had some reason for believing he was in danger. I want to find out why." She *needed* to find out what had led Camille to flee the safety of her new life in Maryland. Whatever it had been, she hadn't felt comfortable confiding it to Shelby, and that hurt, though she would never admit it to Agent Lester. She had worked to keep her friendship with Camille a secret, fearful of being accused of being too personally involved with the witness and transferred off the case.

"Have you found any evidence that the brother really is in danger?"

"No, sir," she admitted. She had tried to keep an eye on Zach and had questioned him and those around him and had uncovered no threat. Which cast a lot of doubt on Camille's motivation to come to Eagle Mountain. Maybe she had just missed her family. "But I'm hoping something on the laptop will clear things up."

"I would have expected her killer to take or destroy the laptop," Lester said.

"Maybe they didn't have time. There were a lot of people at the campground. We have a witness who saw someone suspicious near Camille's van shortly before she died, but the floodwaters were threatening to cut off the camp. He may have decided he needed to leave before he was trapped."

"I read the report," Lester said. "Not a lot of detail to go on." The sound of shuffling papers signaled that Lester had either turned his attention to something else or was growing restless. "I'll give you three more days," he said.

"Thank you, sir." With luck, she would find enough to persuade him to let her stay a week. Her instincts told her the key to this mystery was in Eagle Mountain.

"What's the brother like?" he asked. "The file makes him out to be a drifter. Interesting, considering Camille's degree of focus." Lester had worked the case from the first. He had been one of the agents on the scene immediately after the judge's murder. He had been the first to interview Camille after the Houston Police had contacted the FBI.

"He was grieving his sister's death," she said. "I think he was restless and reluctant to get close to anyone. That seems to have changed here in Eagle Mountain. He has a good job with a mine and is part of the local Search and Rescue team. That takes a lot of commitment."

"Good for him. But is he going to help us bring down the Chalk brothers? Don't lose sight of the mission, Agent Dryden."

"I won't, sir."

"Good. Do what you have to, but wrap things up as soon as you can," he said. "You have plenty of work to do here."

"Yes, sir." She ended the call and sat back on the bed in the plain hotel room that was her headquarters in Eagle Mountain. She had promised Agent Lester that she wouldn't lose sight of her reason for being here. He thought that was to gather as much dirt as she could on the Chalk brothers and their possible connection to Camille's murder.

But Shelby had another mission in mind. She couldn't shake the idea that she had let Camille down. Looking back on her last few conversations with Camille, she could see that her friend had given her hints about what was going on. "I can't stop thinking about Zach," she had said. "I worry about him." Another time, she had asked Shelby what the Chalk brothers would do if a new witness to the judge's murder turned up—say, someone who had been passing by on the street. Would that person be in danger, given that the Chalks had already been acquitted of the murder?

"I think the Chalk brothers wouldn't want to leave anyone out there who could potentially harm them," Shelby had answered. "They might worry prosecutors would come up with new charges. Or the judge's family might file a civil suit. Do you know of another witness? Did you see someone on the street that night?" Shelby searched her friend's face for some sign that Camille was telling the truth or holding back.

"No. I was just playing around with possibilities," Camille said. "I didn't know if the case could go back to trial if a new witness came forward."

"Not if they've been acquitted," Shelby said. "No double jeopardy."

After that, Camille had switched the conversation to talk of a new television series they had both been watching. Only after Camille had vanished did Shelby replay that conversation and berate herself for not digging deeper. Were Camille's renewed worries for her brother and her mention of a potential new witness that night related at all? Was that what got her killed, or was the murder only payback for testifying against the Chalks in the first place?

Objectively, Shelby knew there were plenty of dead ends in investigative work, and many crimes went unsolved for years. But she was determined to do everything she could to discover the reason for Camille's fears about her brother's safety. She hadn't paid enough attention before, and let Camille slip away to face death alone. She didn't want to make that mistake again.

ON TUESDAY AFTERNOON, Zach was called into the human resources office at work. The HR director, Kathleen, was an efficient woman in her mid-forties with a British accent and long, highly polished nails, her brown hair pulled back in a tight chignon. "Zach, how are you doing?" she asked when he settled into the chair across from her desk.

"I'm okay. What did you need to see me about?"

"I was surprised to see you only took three days bereavement leave," she said. "I wanted to make sure you knew you're entitled to longer time off if you feel the need."

He rubbed the back of his neck. "I'm okay," he repeated. "I'd just as soon be at work. Staying busy helps."

Kathleen nodded, though she continued to stare at him as if prepared to dodge out of the way if he suddenly exploded. "If there's anything we can do to help, with navigating the arrangements for your sister's services, or if you need to travel to be with family…"

"We haven't decided anything for certain. I'll let you know." Was all this concern normal, or merely nosiness? "I'd really rather not talk about it," he added.

"Of course." She pressed her lips together. "I am a bit concerned," she said.

"About what?"

"An FBI agent visited this morning. She said she needed to confirm your whereabouts last Monday. I verified that you worked until noon, when you received a call that you were needed to assist Search and Rescue with evacuating a flooded campground, at which time you were excused from your duties here."

He stiffened. "Who was the agent?"

"A woman." She glanced down at the desk, and for the first time, he noticed the business card on the blotter in front of her. "Special Agent Shelby Dryden."

Why was Shelby checking up on him? "What did she say when you told her I was at work?"

"She thanked me and left." Kathleen leaned forward. "What is this about? Are you in trouble with the FBI?"

"No, I'm not in trouble." He gripped the arms of the chair. "Agent Dryden is investigating my sister's death."

Kathleen nodded. "If you need anything, be sure to let us know."

"Thanks." He stood and moved to the door. Instead of returning to his desk, he went out a side door that opened into the parking lot. Sun beat down, the warmth soothing after the air-conditioned chill of the HR office.

He paced, replaying the conversation with Kathleen. Shelby had been at his job? Why?

He pulled out his phone and found the history of her calls to him—calls he hadn't answered. He hit the call back button and she answered after only two rings. "Zach? Is everything all right?"

"No," he said. "I just got called into the HR office and was told that an FBI agent stopped by to verify my whereabouts the day Camille was killed. What was that about?"

"It's just a formality, Zach," she said. "I know you had nothing to do with Camille's death, but I had to eliminate you on paper, that's all."

"I didn't even know Camille was alive!"

"I know, Zach. I'm just dotting all the *i*'s and crossing the *t*'s. When we do find the killer, a good lawyer is going to immediately try to detract attention from their client by pointing the finger at family. Eliminating that possibility up front saves us all trouble in the long run."

He forced himself to breathe more evenly. "One of the Chalk brothers' defense attorneys tried to say Camille killed the judge." He remembered almost coming out of his chair at that moment in the trial. His father had pulled him down.

"No one ever believed that, but it's a way of planting doubt in jurors' minds."

He nodded, even though Shelby couldn't see him. "I would never have hurt Camille," he said. "Never. If only she had contacted me. She could have been safe with me, instead of at that campground."

"Or the person who killed her might have killed you both." Shelby spoke quietly, but he felt the impact of her words. "I'm sorry this happened, Zach," she continued. "Everything about this is ugly. But you and I are on the same side here. We both want justice for Camille."

"Okay." He felt foolish now, blowing up at her. He wasn't one to put his emotions on display. "I have to get back to work now."

"So do I. But call me anytime, even if it's only to complain." He heard the smile behind the words and pictured her pretty, expressive face. "I'm tough. I can take it."

She didn't look tough, but he figured she had to be. Whereas everyone who saw him thought he was strong. They didn't know how wrong they could be.

SHELBY UNDERSTOOD ZACH was annoyed with her for checking his alibi. But she didn't want him to stay annoyed. It was important that he trusted her. She waited until she thought he would be home from work Tuesday and drove to his townhouse. He was just closing the front door behind him when she arrived. "I can't talk now," he said when she approached. "I was just leaving."

"Where are you going?"

He looked for a moment as if he might not answer. Maybe he'd tell her his destination was none of her business. It wasn't as if she hadn't been rebuffed before. "I'm going to pick up dinner," he said.

"Could I come with you?" Before he could object, she continued, "I need to eat, too, and I have information for you about Camille's belongings." Someone with the Marshals Service was already in the process of packing everything to ship to his parents, but she could let him know that was happening. Maybe the thought of having her things would be comforting.

He hesitated, then nodded. "All right."

She could see more of his truck in daytime—the interior cluttered with the belongings of someone who spent a lot of time in his vehicle—an extra jacket, a pack, a water bottle, coffee cups and gas receipts strewn about like confetti. "Where are you staying?" he asked as he turned out of the parking lot.

"I'm at the Ranch Motel."

"I would have thought the feds would spring for something a little more upscale."

"We're on a tight budget, like everyone else these days. But it's not bad. It's clean." She glanced in the side mirror but saw no one behind them.

"No one's following us," he said. "Don't be so paranoid."

Instead of arguing the point, she asked, "What did you order for dinner?"

"Special of the day at the Cakewalk Café—meatloaf, mashed potatoes and green beans."

"Just like Mom used to make?"

"Don't tell my mom, but this is even better."

He parked in front of the neat brick building with white lace curtains showing behind the mullioned windows. Inside, the older woman behind the counter greeted him with a smile. "Hello, Zach. Your order will be out in a few seconds." Then she fixed a questioning smile on Shelby.

"I'd like to get an order to go," she said. "Could I see a menu?"

"Of course." The woman handed over a menu, then left.

She opened the menu, and Zach looked over her shoulder. "It's all good," he said. "They do a great burger."

The woman returned. "Here you are, Zach," she said, and handed a bag over.

Shelby returned the menu. "I'll have the Cobb salad," she said.

"Sure thing. You can have a seat over there to wait." She nodded to a pair of chairs by the door.

She sat, and Zach settled beside her, the bag with his dinner in his lap. "Your food's going to get cold," she said.

He shrugged. "It's all right."

The door opened, and a woman entered. She was tall, her long blond hair in a single braid draped over one shoulder. She looked around and focused on Zach. "Well, hello there," she said, full lips curved in a smile.

She moved closer and rested one hand on his shoulder. "It's so good to see you again."

"Oh, hey." He stood and set the bag with his dinner aside. "It's good to see you, too. How are you?"

"I'm well." Her gaze shifted to Shelby, blue eyes sharp and heavily lined with black liner. Shelby met the gaze but said nothing, even though there was no mistaking the woman's curiosity.

"Your order's ready."

The woman behind the counter summoned Shelby. She paid and collected her order. When she turned around, the blonde was even closer to Zach. "I'll see you later," she said, squeezed his arm and left.

"She didn't stay to eat?" Shelby asked.

Zach stared after her, looking a little dazed. "I guess not."

"Who is she?" Shelby asked.

"A woman I met on a rescue." He picked up his dinner and held the door for Shelby.

"What's her name?" Shelby asked when they were on the sidewalk.

"Janie."

"Janie what?"

"I don't know." He glared at her. "What difference does it make?"

"Where was the rescue?"

"It was that day at the flooded campground. She was one of the campers."

"The day Camille was killed." She still felt a chill at the words. Maybe she always would. "What was she doing here?"

"I don't know. Maybe she saw me through the window and came in to say hello. It was no big deal." He pulled his key fob from his pocket. "Let's go."

"She acted like the two of you were best friends."

"She did not."

"She couldn't stop touching you."

"Some people are like that. You're making a big deal out of nothing."

Maybe she was, but seeing Zach with the blonde had unnerved her. "I'm trying to be careful," she said. "You need to be careful, too."

"You're too suspicious," he said. "I can't live like that."

"You need to be more suspicious if the Chalk brothers are after you."

"Why would they come after me when all this time has passed?"

"You aren't worried that the person who killed your sister will come after you?"

He put the truck in gear and backed out of his parking space. "They don't have any reason to come after me."

"They don't need a reason. Maybe it's enough that your last name is Gregory." How could she make him understand that there were people in this world who were mean for the sake of meanness? They operated by their own code, and her job was to keep them from running over everyone who didn't live by the same code.

He said nothing else on the short drive back to his townhouse. His silence had the weight of anger behind it. The fact that he still didn't trust her hurt, but she couldn't let that interfere with the job she had to do. She slid out of the truck and stood beside him. "You may not want to believe it, but you could be in real danger," she said. "You have to be careful."

"I'll be careful," he said. "But I'm not going to spend my life hiding in my room. And I can't treat everyone I meet as if they're dangerous." Not waiting for an answer, he stalked away, toward his townhouse.

She didn't try to stop him. He wasn't in the mood to listen to anything she had to say. But she needed to make him understand that no matter how much he was used to trusting people, some of them *were* dangerous. And they didn't always reveal that dangerous side until it was too late. She wanted him to believe this, but how could he? He hadn't had her training. In spite of what had happened to Camille, he was still trusting. That was probably a good thing, but it meant she was going to have to work even harder to protect him.

Chapter Nine

Two months ago

The agents who had been around for the Chalk brothers murder trial talked about how cool Camille Gregory had been under pressure. The lead defense attorney, a beefy guy who had gotten as close to the witness box as he could and bellowed his questions, trying to intimidate Camille, got only cool scorn from the state's star witness. "What I want to know, Ms. Gregory, is what someone like you—a waitress—has to gain from testifying against powerful men like my clients. Who put you up to this?"

"I've always had a strong sense of justice," Camille said, looking him in the eye and not blinking. "But maybe you missed that class when you went to law school."

The courtroom came apart at that, and the judge had to pound his gavel and admonish the witness to stick to answering the question. But Camille wasn't cowed. "Was that a question?" she asked. "It sounded to me like an accusation."

The media had loved her. Countless articles referred to her as a "brave young woman." If she was losing sleep under the strain of the trial, she never showed it, those veteran agents told Shelby when she was first assigned to question Camille.

But Shelby had seen a softer side of her friend. One who confided that she spent more than one break during her testimony in the ladies' room throwing up from the stress of it all. And even though she had been upset that the Chalk brothers had gotten away with murder, part of her was relieved to have that ordeal past her. She had focused on building a new life for herself and doing all she could to protect her family.

So when Shelby visited Camille one Saturday afternoon for a "girls' night" of wine and videos and noticed the circles under Camille's eyes and the chips in her manicure, Shelby knew something was up. "What's wrong?" she asked as she watched Camille fumbling to open a wine bottle.

"Nothing's wrong." Camille tried to smile but couldn't force the expression into her eyes.

Shelby snagged one hand and pointed to the mangled manicure. "Has someone else been picking at your nails, then?"

Camille pulled her hand away. "It's nothing."

"If you're upset, it's something."

"I don't want to get into trouble." She wrestled the cap off the wine and filled two glasses.

"Tell me, and we'll figure it out together."

Camille set aside the bottle but didn't pick up her wine glass. Shelby waited, the silence stretched between them. She was better at this game than Camille and knew it.

"I know I'm not supposed to go on social media," Camille began.

Again, Shelby said nothing. She sipped the wine, gaze fixed on Camille.

"I opened an account. Not under my own name. And I never post. I'm just on Facebook and Insta and a few other places, to see what my old friends are up to."

Shelby wasn't surprised. She hadn't worked much with witness security, but she couldn't imagine Camille was the first person to break the no-social-media rule. "What name are you under?" she asked.

"Gladys Grunch." Camille wrinkled her nose.

Shelby pulled out her phone, opened the Instagram app and found the account. No posts, as Camille had said. She checked Facebook. Same. "This doesn't look bad," she said. "The cybersecurity people will want to take a look. They can set it up so the account can't be traced back to you."

Camille picked up her wine glass. "Okay."

Shelby laid aside her phone. "What's the problem?" she asked. "What has you upset?"

"A woman I worked with at Britannia—Amy—posted the other day that a man came into the restaurant, asking about the night Judge Hennessey was murdered. At first, she thought maybe he was a reporter and told him she didn't want to talk about it. Then he said he wasn't a reporter, that he worked for the Chalk brothers. He said they had hired him to find out what had really happened that night. He said the Chalk brothers wanted to clear their name."

"Maybe they did hire someone," Shelby said. "We can look into it."

"That's not what upset me," Camille said. "It's that he told her the Chalk brothers believe someone else was at the pub that night, with me. They found out my car was in the shop that night and thought maybe my brother gave me a lift to work and picked me up, so he might have seen something." She set the wine glass down hard enough that some of the liquid sloshed onto the counter. "Zach wasn't there. I took the bus that night. But if the Chalk brothers believe he was, they might hurt him."

"We'll check out this guy and see what we can find out," Shelby said. "And we'll alert local law enforcement to keep an eye on Zach."

Camille nodded and picked up the wine again. "This place Zach is living—Eagle Mountain. Have you ever been there?"

"No."

"I looked it up online," Shelby said. "It's pretty. Really small, in the mountains. They don't have a traffic light or a single chain store. Hard to imagine."

"I would think it would be harder for a stranger to blend in, in a place like that," Shelby said. "And easier for the local cops to make sure Zach is all right."

"I guess it's silly for me to worry after all this time," Camille said. "I mean, Zach doesn't have anything to do with the Chalk brothers or Judge Hennessey's murder or anything. He's moved on with his life and probably doesn't even think about me."

"Your family hasn't forgotten you," Shelby said. "How could they?"

Camille shrugged and drained her glass. "It's hard," she whispered.

"Hard to be without them," Shelby said.

"That. But it's harder to know I can't protect them. Before, during the trial, I could still keep an eye on them, and there were cops everywhere to look out for them. Then, when it came time for me to leave, I knew that staying away from them was the best way to protect them. Knowing that what I was doing was helping them kept me going those first difficult months. But when I read Amy's post online, I realized how vulnerable they still are. And how helpless I am." Her eyes met Shelby's, shiny with unshed tears. "They shouldn't have to suffer for what I did," she said. "That was never what I wanted."

Shelby put her hand on her friend's. "I know," she said. "I promise, we're still looking out for them."

Camille looked down into her empty glass. "Zach looks tough, but he has such a soft heart," she said. "He could never have stood up to what the Chalk brothers put me through. I think to deal with really bad people like that you have to be a little bad yourself."

"You're not bad," Shelby said.

"Only when I have to be." She smiled, and some of the sadness lifted. "I feel better now, talking to you. Now let's pick out a movie. I'm in the mood for something sappy and romantic. How about you?"

Shelby would have liked to talk more, but she knew when to surrender to Camille. The moment of vulnerability had passed, and the impervious Camille was back in charge. The woman who had made up her mind and wouldn't back down.

ELDON AND ZACH met in the Zenith Mine parking lot after work on Wednesday and drove together in Zach's truck to Caspar Canyon. With the summer solstice approaching, the days were long enough to allow plenty of hours of good light for climbing the many designated routes on the canyon's granite walls. They shouldered their gear, and Eldon led the way into the canyon. They passed other climbers along the way, many of whom called out to Eldon in greeting. "Do you know everybody?" Zach asked after the sixth time they stopped to chat with another climber.

"This is a small town," Eldon said. "Sooner or later you do feel like you know everyone. But the climbing community is especially close."

"How long have you lived here?" Zach asked.

"A little over two years. How about you?"

"Nine months," Zach said.

"You'll be an old-timer in no time." They stopped beside an empty section of canyon wall that towered thirty feet overhead. Smooth rock in shades of caramel, red, gold and cream reminded Zach of melted candle wax—and looked almost as slick. "This is a good beginner pitch," Eldon said. "Let's get our gear set up."

Zach studied the wall again. It wasn't perfectly vertical, but almost, and while permanent pins studded the wall like cloves in a ham, nothing about this said "beginner" to him. "I really haven't climbed much at all," he said as he unfolded his harness. "Just a couple of times during SAR training."

"That's all you need for this pitch," Eldon said. "Trust me."

Helmets and harnesses in place, Eldon reviewed the basics. Then he turned to the wall. "I'd start right there. See that handhold? Grab hold of that, then you can put your foot right there. See where the rock juts out a little.

Perfect step. From there, you should be able to reach that little lip to the left. See it?"

Zach looked closer, and he began to notice not smooth wall, but dozens of little divots and protrusions. Enough for a hand- or foothold. Still, he had to be strong enough to make his way up the wall without losing his balance. "What if I miss a hold or lean back too far?" he asked.

"The rope will catch you." He indicated the belay ropes stretched out between them. "I'll climb up first and set this, then you come up after. Don't worry. It will be just like walking up a ladder."

Eldon went up first, without a rope. He easily scaled the wall, moving so quickly Zach didn't have time to make note of every place he put his hands or feet. He anchored the rope and tossed the end down to Zach, who fastened it to his harness as he had learned in SAR training. Then he rubbed his hands together, took a deep breath. "You can do this," he muttered, and started up.

Eldon had lied, he decided after he had hauled himself up the first few feet. This wasn't as easy as climbing a ladder. But it wasn't impossible. And as long as he avoided looking down and focused on carefully choosing his next handhold or his next step up, he could do this. His muscles protested and shook with strain by the time he reached the top, but he didn't freeze or freak out. He was grinning by the time he stood beside Eldon at the canyon rim.

"That was great." Eldon slapped him on the back. "How did it feel?"

"It felt good." He rolled his shoulders. "I felt…strong."

"Didn't I tell you? You may have more bulk to haul

up here, but you have the muscle to do it. Did you play football in high school?"

"Left tackle." Ages ago.

"Same here," Eldon said. "Climbing beats crashing into people on the field any day, in my book."

They spent the next two hours climbing in a couple of different areas. In between climbs, they discovered surprisingly similar backgrounds. Eldon was from Hawaii, but like Zach, he had grown up with one sister. She was married with kids in Hawaii. "My whole family can't understand why I would ever leave the islands," he said. "I miss them all, but I'm happier here. I just fit in better here, you know?"

Zach nodded. He was beginning to feel that way, too. He loved his parents, but he was glad they had moved away from Houston. That city held too many reminders of Camille. Here in the mountains they could all start fresh.

Had Camille felt that when she moved to Maryland? She had truly started over, with a new name, a new backstory. Had she gotten to choose the details herself, or had the Marshals Service assigned her a role? Either way, she would have relished playing this new part. She had always enjoyed being the life of the party or the star of the show.

The sun was setting when they packed up their gear and headed back to Zach's truck. They were loading up when someone hailed them from across the parking lot. "Hey!"

They turned and saw a tall blond loping toward them. "Remember me?" the man asked. "Todd. You two were part of the Search and Rescue team that took care of me when I rolled my ATV last week."

"Todd with two Ds," Eldon said. "How are you doing?"

"I'm good." He pointed to the fading cut on the side of his head. "This is almost healed up." He nodded toward their gear bags. "So you guys been doing some climbing?"

No, we just carry this stuff around to look good, Zach thought. Instead, he said, "Do you climb?"

"I've been thinking about getting into it. I just came out here to watch. Say, I owe you guys a beer. Want to go somewhere and grab a drink?"

Eldon looked at Zach. "Sound okay to you?"

Zach shrugged. "Sure, why not?" He wasn't going to turn down a free beer, and it wasn't as if he had anything else planned for that evening.

"You can follow us to Mo's Pub," Eldon said. "Do you know where that is?"

Todd grinned. "It's my new favorite place. Let me help you with your gear." He bent and picked up Zach's gear bag, grunting with the effort.

"I'll get it." Zach stepped in and took the bag from Todd.

Todd slapped him on the back. "Guess I'd better leave the heavy lifting to the real mountain man." He followed them to the parking area, then waved. "See you at Mo's," he said, and loped toward a white sedan.

"You don't mind having a drink or two with this guy, do you?" Eldon asked when he and Zach were alone in Zach's truck.

"It's okay," Zach said. "He seems nice enough."

"He'll probably want to hear search and rescue stories,"

Eldon said. "He had that look. But we only have to stay for one drink if he's too much."

"I'm good," Zach said. Normally, he wouldn't spend time with someone he didn't know, but he was trying to be more sociable since moving to Eagle Mountain. He wanted to stay here awhile, and that meant fitting in with the community.

Mo's Pub was busy with a midweek crowd. Drinkers filled the stools around the L-shaped bar, a baseball game showing on the TVs overhead. The three men found a booth along one side and ordered beers. "So what brings you to Eagle Mountain?" Eldon asked Todd.

"Oh, you know, the scenery. The outdoors. I live in Denver and wanted to get away from the city for a few days. I'd never been here before and thought I'd take a look." He turned to Zach. "What about you guys? Have you lived here long?"

"A little while," Zach said.

"I can see why someone would want to settle down here," Todd said. "I really like the vibe of the place. Are there any good jobs? Where do you work?" He glanced at Eldon, then focused on Zach once more. His laser focus made Zach uncomfortable. Why was this guy asking so many questions?

"We work at the Zenith gold mine," Eldon said.

"A gold mine? No kidding? What do you do there?"

"Nothing exciting," Zach said before Eldon could answer. They were never going to see this guy again, so there was no need to tell their life stories.

"Zach Gregory." Todd said the name as if trying it out. "Are you related to that woman who was killed during the flood at that campground early last week?"

"How did you know about that?" Zach asked.

"I read about it in the paper. Was she a relative of yours?"

"She was my sister." He kept his voice flat, hoping Todd would get the message that this wasn't something Zach wanted to discuss.

"Hey, I didn't know. I'm sorry." Todd shook his head. "That must have been rough. What happened to her? The paper said a tree fell on her van."

Zach met Todd's eyes with a hard stare. Apparently, this guy couldn't take a hint. "I don't want to talk about it," he said.

"Yeah, I get it." Todd nodded, then opened his mouth, as if to ask another nosy question.

"What happened with your rental ATV?" Eldon asked, and Zach was grateful to him for changing the subject. "They didn't ding you too much for the damage, did they?"

"Three hundred bucks." Todd winced. "But I guess it's going to cost that much to knock out the dents. That's what I get for going too fast on those rough trails." He turned back to Zach. "My sister died a few years ago," he said. "So I know how you feel."

I doubt it, Zach thought. "I'm sorry to hear that," he said.

"Yeah. She was shot in a drive-by shooting. They never did find out who killed her. That's hard, you know? No closure."

Zach stared. Was this guy telling the truth? How much did he know about Camille's death? Zach hadn't read the article in the paper, so he didn't know how much it said. Maybe he should find a copy and read it. Or he could ask Shelby.

"Zach!"

He jerked his head up to see a familiar woman working her way through the crowd toward them. More than one man's head turned to watch her as she passed. The tall blonde wore formfitting jeans and a black, low-cut sleeveless top that showed off an impressive figure. Zach stood as she approached the booth. "Hey, Janie," he said, aware of Eldon and Todd staring.

"Hey, there," she said, and leaned in to give him a big hug.

When they separated, Eldon was grinning, and Todd was frowning. "I don't mean to intrude," she said, "but I've been looking all over town for you." She kept one hand on his arm, her hip brushing the top of his thigh. She was tall for a woman, close to six feet, and he felt less like a giant next to her. "I wanted to say thank you again." She looked at the vacant seat next to Zach.

"Sit down," he said, moving over to make room.

"I'd better go," Todd said. "It was good to see you guys again." He slid out of the booth and hurried away.

"I didn't mean to scare off your friend," Janie said as she slid into the booth next to Zach. She sat close, almost touching him.

"It's okay," Zach said. "Um, Eldon, this is Janie. She was one of the campers we evacuated from the Piñon Creek campground."

"I remember." Eldon was still grinning.

"It's nice to see you again, too." She offered him her hand. Her nails were painted pale blue, and her bare arms were tanned, as if she'd spent a week at the beach.

They shook hands. "Where are you from?" he asked.

"I'm from a little town outside of Houston," she said.

"I'm from Houston," Zach said.

He felt the impact of her smile again, heating him up from the inside. "It's a small world, isn't it?" she said.

Houston was a big city, and lots of people from Texas visited Colorado, so it wasn't so surprising he should run into someone from near his hometown. Still, it was a little connection between them. "Would you like a drink?" Zach asked.

"Oh, just a Diet Coke." She hit him with the full force of her smile—white teeth, generous pink lips and brilliant blue eyes that sparkled.

The server arrived, and she ordered a Diet Coke, while he and Eldon asked for two more beers. "Did our friend pick up the tab for the first round?" Eldon asked.

"'Fraid not," said their server, a redhead named Kiki.

"I figured," Eldon said.

"Some friend," Kiki said, and sauntered away.

"You should let me pay," Janie said. "Since I sort of ran him off."

"Don't worry about it," Zach said.

"Are you camping by yourself?" Eldon asked. "Or with friends? A boyfriend?" He smirked at Zach.

"Just some friends." She smiled at Kiki as the server set a glass of Diet Coke in front of her, along with Zach's and Eldon's beers. "Thanks." She sipped the drink, then added, "Actually, they left today to head out to Moab. I decided to stick around a few more days." She moved her leg so that she brushed against Zach. "I was hoping I'd run into you again."

"Uh, yeah. It's good to see you again, too." He sipped

his beer, aware of her still touching him. He was flattered by her attention, but why was she coming on so strong? She didn't know anything about him. And all he knew about her was that she was gorgeous and not at all shy.

"How long have you two volunteered with Search and Rescue?" she asked, including Eldon in the conversation.

"A couple of years," Eldon said. "Zach is still a rookie."

"It's really amazing that you give so much of your time and energy to helping others," she said.

"It's a pretty amazing group," Eldon said.

Janie was still looking at Eldon, but her hand was stroking Zach's thigh. Maybe this wasn't even happening. Maybe it was a dream. Any minute now, firefighters would rush in and start spraying him down with a fire hose, or the server would show up with a live duck on a silver tray, or some other bizarre thing would occur to let him know that he definitely wasn't in the real world anymore.

"Now this is interesting," Eldon said. He was looking over Zach's shoulder.

Zach turned his head to see Shelby striding toward them. Like Janie, she was dressed in jeans, but she also wore a light jacket and a grim expression. She stopped beside the table, and her gaze flicked over Eldon and Janie before settling on Zach. "We need to talk," she said.

"Zach's a little busy right now," Janie said. Her voice was pleasant enough, but Zach still flinched at the look she directed at Shelby. He half expected to smell singed hair.

"Janie, this is Shelby," Zach said. "Shelby, this is Janie."

"Agent Shelby Dryden, FBI," Shelby said.

Janie laughed. "Oh, that's funny," she said. "I thought maybe you were Zach's ex-girlfriend or something." She turned to Zach. "But what does a fed want with you?"

"Zach is a potential witness in an investigation I'm involved in," Shelby said. She looked less sure of herself now. She turned to Zach. "I didn't mean to interrupt. But get in touch with me as soon as you can. I may have found something."

"Really? On Camille's laptop?"

She frowned and shook her head. "We'll talk later." With another glance at Janie, she pivoted and left.

Janie leaned in even closer to Zach. "Now that was interesting! You helping the feds? What was that all about? Who's Camille?"

"It's a long story." What had Shelby found that she needed him to see? Was it a clue as to who had killed Camille, or something else?

"I'm gonna call it a night." Eldon pulled out a wallet and tossed a twenty on the table. "That ought to cover my half of the tab."

"I need to go, too," Zach said. He forced a smile and turned to Janie. "It was good seeing you again."

"You don't have to say goodbye yet." She looped her arm in his. "Maybe we could go back to my place?"

Eldon made a choking sound, as if he was trying— and failing—to hold back laughter, either over Janie's heavy-handed seduction or Zach's obvious discomfort. Zach freed his arm. "Thanks, but I really do need to go."

She pouted, but it was such a put-on look he couldn't take it seriously. He saw Kiki headed their way and raised his hand. "We need to settle up," he said.

They paid their bill, and Janie reluctantly moved over and let Zach out of the booth. "I'm sure we'll see each other again," she said, and threw her arms around him. He froze, and when she stretched up as if to kiss him, he turned his head so that her lips brushed his cheek. He mumbled goodbye, then moved past her and out of the restaurant.

Outside, he remembered that Eldon had ridden with him. He waited until his friend emerged from the restaurant. "I was half afraid you were going to drive off without me," Eldon said as he slid into the passenger seat. "You were in a hurry to get out of there."

"Sorry," Zach said. "I wanted to get away from Janie."

"That wasn't what I expected when we decided to stop off for a beer," Eldon said.

"All I did was help with a rescue. I don't know why she was coming on so strong."

"She obviously has the hots for you," Eldon said. "But you can't complain about having two good looking women pursuing you."

"Agent Dryden's 'pursuit' isn't exactly the kind most people want," Zach said. "And Janie is gorgeous, but she's a little over-the-top, don't you think?"

"Over-the-top can be good," Eldon said. "But I know what you mean. She came across as kind of fake. The attitude, anyway. I don't know about the rest of her."

Zach nodded and blew out a breath. "I don't have the energy to deal with her right now."

"What about Agent Dryden?" Eldon asked.

"I'll call her when I get back to my place. She's here investigating my sister's murder. Maybe she's found something."

"That's got to be rough," Eldon said. "I couldn't believe Todd kept going on about that, even after you let him know you didn't want to talk about it."

"Some people are just socially awkward," Zach said. "I don't think he meant any harm. Does that happen often? People you rescue glomming onto you afterward?"

"I've never run into it personally, though I've heard stories about Search and Rescue groupies who pursue volunteers. But most people are just grateful and not pushy. I had a guy buy my dinner once when he saw me in a restaurant, but it was all very low-key. He didn't try to be my new best friend or learn my life story. And I never had a woman come on to me the way Janie did you."

"A groupie, huh?" He shrugged. "I don't get it, but whatever." He glanced at Eldon. "Are you seeing anyone?"

"Yeah. May is a local artist. We met when she worked at the coffee shop. Kind of an ordinary way to meet, I guess."

"Ordinary is good," Zach said. Ordinary wasn't something he had had much of in his life since Camille had returned to the restaurant that night. How could life be ordinary again, when he had a sister who had died twice and a file with the FBI with his name on it?

Chapter Ten

Shelby paced back and forth in the small space between the bed and the door in her hotel room. She had handled this evening with Zach all wrong. When she had spotted the message on Camille's laptop, she had been so anxious to figure out what it meant that she had contacted him right away. But his phone had gone to voicemail, and he hadn't answered her texts. She had started to drive to his townhouse, but when she passed Mo's Pub, she saw his truck parked at the curb and decided to go inside.

That was wrong move number one. Number two was marching up to the booth where he sat with the big Hawaiian dude from Search and Rescue and that blonde beauty queen who practically had blue fire shooting out of her eyes when Shelby had dared to talk to Zach. Where had she come from? Though Zach had never answered her question about whether or not he was involved with someone, her own discreet checking had indicated he was still pretty much a loner. And though he and the blonde—Janie—had been sitting very close together, she had sensed that Zach wasn't all that happy about it. But maybe she had been reading him wrong, and what he was really unhappy about was her intruding on his evening.

Mistake number three was giving Zach the chance to say anything about Camille or the laptop in public. She would have been smarter to wait until he returned her call or text and arrange a meeting at a later date and time. Now she just felt foolish and out of sorts.

Who was that woman? There was nothing in Zach's file about anyone named Janie. He said he had met her at the campground the day Camille died, but was that true? And now she was back in Eagle Mountain, cozying up to him in that booth at Mo's.

As soon as Camille had mentioned she was worried about her brother, Shelby had begun gathering as much information as possible about Zach, and she hadn't run into any mention of Janie or any other woman in his life. She had told herself she was doing it in order to reassure Camille that he was safe, but as weeks passed, Shelby had to admit she became more and more interested in the "big bear," as Camille referred to him. The information she had been able to glean had formed a picture of a quiet, intelligent, hurting man who was struggling to recover from the trauma of losing his sister and rebuild his life.

He was struggling, but he was winning the struggle, she had told Camille. Some people never got over tragedy in their lives, but Zach was stronger than most, physically as well as mentally. Shelby had found herself silently rooting for him when she realized he was staying put in Eagle Mountain longer than any other place he had lived in the past four years. He was part of a community here. He had friends. He was going to be all right.

She ought to be happy he was dating again. Camille would have been. But seeing him with that woman, who was crowding him in the booth as if she wanted to keep him from running away, had unsettled her. Why?

A knock on the door startled her. She froze. Who would be knocking on her door this time of night? The knock came again. "Shelby, are you in there? It's me, Zach."

She let out a breath, then checked the security peep. Zach stood in front of the door, hands shoved in the pockets of his jeans, bouncing on the balls of his feet like a boxer in the ring before the bell sounded. She unfastened the chain and the dead bolt and opened the door. "How did you know which room was mine?" she asked.

"I didn't. I knocked on all the doors on this floor until a guy told me you were in this room."

So much for security. She opened the door wider and let him in. "You didn't have to break off your date," she said. "This could have waited until morning."

"It wasn't a date," he said.

"Oh?"

"Eldon and I went climbing and stopped by Mo's for a beer and ran into Janie. You remember, I told you she was one of the people we helped evacuate from the flood last week." He froze, then swore. "She was at the campground with Camille. I should have asked her if she saw Camille. Maybe she spoke to her. Or maybe she saw someone with her…"

"The sheriff's deputies interviewed all the other campers," Shelby said. "Camille kept to herself and didn't speak to any of them except one man who made a point of speaking to her. He was the only one who saw anyone near her camp."

He still looked stricken. "Still, I should have asked.

I was so taken aback by the way she was coming on to me." He flushed.

"She was coming on to you?" Shelby's conscience told her this was none of her business, but this information—and Zach's obvious distress—intrigued her.

"She was just…really grateful," he said.

"Does that happen very often?" she asked. "Grateful women throwing themselves at you?"

He laughed, though there was no mirth in the sound. "Never. And Eldon says it's never happened to him."

"She was very pretty." *In an overdone kind of way*, Shelby silently added. Was that catty of her? Maybe.

"I don't even know her." He straightened his shoulders. "I guess I prefer it if a woman lets me do at least a little pursuing. Or at least if the attraction leads to something mutual."

"You're not one for a one-night stand?"

Again the flush. It made him look boyish. "Let's just say I like to know a woman longer than ten minutes before we decide to go home together."

"I shouldn't have interrupted you," she said. "I apologize."

"No. It's okay. What did you need to talk to me about?"

She looked around for somewhere for them both to sit. The room contained only one chair and a table so small they would have difficulty both sitting at it. She settled for the end of the bed. She sat and indicated the spot beside her. "I want you to take a look at something on Camille's laptop."

The mattress dipped beneath his weight as he settled beside her, and she braced one foot on the floor to keep from sliding into him. Why did the fact that they were sitting on a bed and not a sofa feel so much more intimate? She pushed aside the thought and booted up the laptop.

"Our forensic experts will take a look at this more closely when I send it in," she said. "I'm just doing a quick scan to see if there's anything that seems significant right away. What I'm going to show you caught my attention, but I don't know if it means anything." The password screen opened, and she typed in *CMONKEY1016*, and the home screen loaded.

"How did you know her password?" he asked.

"The background of her password screen is of sea monkeys," she said. "October 16 is the night Judge Hennessey was murdered."

"The night that changed her life," he said. "Still, I probably wouldn't have figured out her password."

"The two of us spent a lot of time together. I knew how she thought." About some things, anyway. She hadn't realized Camille planned to leave WITSEC and head to Colorado until it was too late.

She opened a file labeled MeOhMy. "This was the first thing that caught my attention." She angled the computer so Zach could read the screen. "She's keeping kind of a journal here. This first entry explains her intentions. Read it, then I'll take you to the entry I need your help with."

She reread the entry along with Zach: *I'm starting this journal as a place to write down my thoughts and maybe make sense of some things. I figure it's better to put it here than on paper. If I write for long, my hand cramps, and if I need to, I can easily erase this file and even destroy the whole computer. Phillip showed me how to do that, in a way that no data can be discovered.*

"Who's Phillip?" Zach asked.

"He was the marshal she was involved with. None of the entries are dated, but move to the third entry."

He scrolled down to the entry in question: *I watched an interview online with Charlie Chalk. It was an old one, filmed not long after his and Christopher's trial ended, but I had never seen it before. Something he said made my blood freeze. He said, "There were other people involved that night, and they're the ones who will pay."*

I kept running the video back to replay that part. Maybe he was trying to imply that someone else—a third person—killed Judge Hennessey. That's what his defense team said all along. But Charlie knows that isn't true. So maybe he meant someone else was there that night. And the Chalk brothers are the ones who will make that person pay.

Claude, are you safe? Do you even know how to be safe? I've learned so much in the past four years. Mostly what I've learned is how naive I was before. I thought I had taken care of everything, but maybe I was wrong.

"Who is Claude?" she asked.

He shook his head. "I don't know."

But he wouldn't meet her gaze, and his face had lost most of its color. She carefully set the laptop aside and angled toward him. "Don't lie to me, Zach. I'm being honest with you. I didn't have to share any of this with you, but I did. All I ask is the same consideration in turn."

He stood, everything in his body language telling her he wanted to flee. "She didn't have any friends or coworkers named Claude." He shoved his hands in his jeans pockets and stared at the floor.

"There are other entries in here where the names have obviously been changed," Shelby said. She struggled to keep her voice even, though she wanted to shout at him that she wasn't oblivious—and that he was a terrible liar. "I think *Claude* is a code name, or maybe a nickname. And I think you know who she's talking about. Whose safety is she so worried about, and why?"

He stiffened, hands knotted in fists, jaw tightening, doing battle with himself. She waited, silently willing him to trust her with the truth. After a long, tense moment, he blew out a breath. "She called me Claude sometimes," he said. "There's a bear at the Houston Zoo with that name, and she teased me that I looked like him. But I don't know why she was worried about me."

"That's a sweet story, not an embarrassing one," she said. "Thank you for telling me."

He still looked miserable. Out of proportion for what had been a pretty innocuous revelation. "What about the other stuff she wrote?" he asked. "Do the Chalk brothers think someone else was at the restaurant the night Judge Hennessey was killed? Are they telling the truth about a third man who was the actual murderer?"

"We've looked into the theory and found nothing to support it." She stood and went to face him. She needed to ask the question she should have asked long before now. "We know Shelby's car was in the shop for repairs the night Judge Hennessey was murdered," she said. "One of her coworkers said that you sometimes picked her up from work when her car wasn't available."

"She took the bus," he said. "She told you that."

"That's what she told us, but is it true? Did you pick her up from Britannia that night? Were you there? Did you see what happened? Is that why Camille was so worried about you? She heard the Chalk brothers were saying someone else was there that night and vowing to make that person pay? Were you that person?"

He grimaced as if in physical pain. "I didn't see the murder," he said. "I was waiting for her outside."

Some part of her had known this would be his answer. "All those times Camille insisted that she was alone at Britannia that night never rang all the way true for me," she said. "She put such emphasis on that one fact—she was by herself, she was alone, she was the only one to hear that gunshot—it was too much. But at the time of the initial investigation, before my time with the Bureau, no one ever doubted her or bothered to collect evidence to prove or disprove her assertion."

"She insisted that since hers was the only testimony needed to prove the Chalk brothers had murdered Judge Hennessey, there was no point putting myself in danger," he said. "She said our parents didn't need two children involved in that kind of danger. And…and I guess it was easier for me to agree with her." He looked away. "She was the brave one. I was a coward, letting her face that alone."

His pain pierced her. She took hold of his arm. "Camille wanted to do it alone," she said. "She may have wanted to protect you and her parents, too, but I think at least part of her didn't want to share the attention."

His gaze met hers, and the gratitude that burned there washed over her. "You really did know her, didn't you?"

"Yes." She told herself she ought to let go of him, but

the physical connection between them felt too good to relinquish. "Camille liked the attention and praise she got for testifying against the Chalk brothers. I don't blame her for that. What she did was important and good. But I don't think she wanted to share that spotlight."

"Would it have made any difference if I had testified that I sat outside in my truck and waited for her?" he asked.

"I don't think so."

He put his hand over hers on his arm. He touched her hand, but she felt the sensation all through her body, warming her. Making her feel more alive. The contact only lasted a second but seemed much longer as she stared into his eyes.

Then he lifted her hand away and stepped back, breaking the contact. "I'd better go," he said.

She nodded. She didn't want him to leave, but he was right. Nothing good would come of him staying. "Thank you for telling me the truth," she said.

"I'm sorry I didn't say something before. Maybe if I had, Camille would still be alive."

"You can't know that. She liked taking risks. Maybe she was growing bored in WITSEC. If she hadn't decided to leave protection to see you, she might have found some other excuse. She wouldn't be the first person to take that kind of risk simply for the thrill. When you've been at the center of such intense excitement for years, a normal life must seem very dull."

She couldn't tell from his expression whether he believed her or not. "Good night," he said, and walked out.

She locked the door behind him, then pressed her forehead to the cool metal of the door. Her hand was still warm where he had touched her. That one moment of intense chemistry had been such a rush. She shouldn't have let it happen, but she could never regret it. Camille wasn't the only person in this mess who liked to live dangerously.

Four years ago

"WE FIND THE defendants not guilty."

Zach didn't hear the next words. Not because the crowd erupted into shouts, the judge slamming down his gavel to restore order. Zach didn't hear because the white noise of confusion filled his head. How could this be happening? Camille had been inside the Britannia Pub the night Judge Andrew Hennessey was murdered. She had heard the shot and looked into the dining room to see Charlie and Christopher Chalk standing over the dying man. She had testified to everything she had seen, not wavering when the Chalk brothers' lawyer tried to bully her and practically accused her of lying.

He had never been more proud than he had been when seeing his sister seated in the witness box, head up and back straight, telling her story with no sign of fear, though the dark eyes of the Chalk brothers bored into her.

But something had gone wrong. The Chalk brothers weren't going to prison for the rest of their lives. They were going to walk away from the courthouse as free men.

"What went wrong?" He lunged forward and grabbed the arm of the lead prosecutor as the man turned to leave the courtroom.

The man glared and shook him off. "No comment," he said, and walked away.

Zach looked around the room for his parents, from whom he had become separated in the chaos after the verdict was announced. He spotted the back of his father's head amid a sea of reporters wielding microphones and cameras, and bulled his way through the crowd to him. "How do you feel, knowing your daughter risked her life for nothing?" a man in a stylish blue suit and dark glasses asked as he thrust a microphone in Zach's mother's face.

Zach leaned forward and shoved the microphone away, then put his arm around his mother. "Come on, Mom," he said. "Let's get out of here."

The surrounding reporters raised their voices, firing more questions. "No comment!" Zach all but shouted, then steered his parents away.

Two FBI agents emerged out of nowhere and herded Zach and his parents into an elevator and upstairs. "Where are you taking us?" Zach's mother asked, but neither of the feds answered—two men in identical dark blue suits, with identical grim expressions.

They led the way to a door and opened it. Zach filed in after his parents, and Camille embraced them. She was pale, her eyes swollen and reddened, as if she had been crying. The prosecutor was there, too, looking less grim than before.

"What happened?" The question came from Zach's dad now. His father, who was only fifty, was looking ten years older, his shoulders stooped, his hair thinning at the back.

"The defense team planted enough doubt that the jury failed to convict," the prosecutor—a man named Zable—said.

"But I was there," Camille said. "I saw the Chalk

brothers standing over the judge's body seconds after that gunshot."

"But you didn't see the gun or see them pull the trigger."

Zach had heard the defense team make the argument that because Camille hadn't witnessed the moment the bullet was fired, the jury couldn't say with 100 percent certainty that the Chalk brothers had killed the judge. Their contention was that someone else had run in and fired that fatal shot while the Chalk brothers were meeting with the judge. Zach hadn't thought anyone would believe that theory.

"Can you appeal?" he asked. "Ask for a new trial?"

"Not on a murder charge," the prosecutor said. "Once a person is declared not guilty of murder, they can't be tried again. Our constitution prohibits double jeopardy."

Zach's dad stood with his arm around his daughter. "What happens now?" he asked.

The prosecutor and the two agents looked at Camille. She eased away from her father. "It's going to be okay, Dad," she said. "I'm going to have police protection for a little while longer, just to make sure I'm okay."

"Is she going to be okay?" His father addressed the agents. "These men are killers. Thugs. They know who Camille is and that she testified against them. What's to keep them from going after her?"

"We have a lot of experience protecting witnesses," one of the agents—the one with the grayer hair—said. "You don't need to worry." He turned to Camille. "You need to say goodbye so that we can leave."

She blinked rapidly, as if fighting tears, then moved

over to Zach and hugged him tightly. "Don't say anything to anyone," she whispered. "Promise me."

"I already promised," he said.

"Promise me again."

He said nothing. "What's going on? What's really
going to happen?"

"I have to lie low for a little bit, that's all." She forced
a smile, but her eyes were bleak. She stepped back. "I'll
be okay. You look after Mom and Dad and remember
what we talked about."

You weren't there. You didn't see anything. Except he
had. He agreed with Camille that what he had seen probably didn't mean anything and wouldn't have made a difference in the outcome of the trial. But he hated that he
had let her talk him into silence. She thought she knew
what was best, but what if she was wrong?

"We have to go," someone said.

Camille straightened her shoulders and fixed her
smile more firmly in place. "I love you all," she said.
"Don't worry about me. I'll be fine."

The door opened, and she left the room, though Zach
could scarcely see her in the crowd of men who surrounded her. He caught a glimpse of pink from the dress
she wore, showing in the midst of a wall of dark suits.

He didn't know that would be the last time he would
see his sister alive. Or that four years later, what had happened at the Britannia Pub would still be tearing at him.

ZACH DROVE WITH the windows open, letting the cool night
air help clear his muddled thinking. Shelby had thanked
him for telling her the truth, but he hadn't told her everything. He hadn't mentioned the man who ran into

the street shortly before Camille exited the building. He knew he should have said something, but so many years of keeping secrets made it hard to get the words out. It was almost as if he thought he would be dishonoring his sister by revealing what he had promised to keep secret. The Chalk brothers wanted Judge Hennessey dead. They had killed him. Whoever that third man was, he didn't have anything to do with the crime. He was probably some street person, running from the sound of gunfire.

At least Shelby knew part of his secret. She knew he had been waiting for Camille the night of the murder. Even revealing that bit of truth had felt good, like letting off the pressure of a too tight tourniquet. That had to explain his response to her, that moment of electricity when he had fought not to pull her close.

The intensity of the moment had caught him off-guard, though he had been aware of a sexual tension between them from the moment he walked into her hotel room. He had put it down to the aftereffects of Janie's attempted seduction. Shelby was an attractive woman, but she was also an FBI agent who was investigating his sister's murder. She wasn't interested in Zach as a man. Still, he had spent the hour or so he was in that room breathing in the soft floral scent of her perfume, noticing the way her hair curled around her cheek and the softness of her arm as she brushed against him as she typed on the keyboard.

And then she took hold of his arm, and he felt the connection. He had wanted that touch and more. Whether it was frustration or relief or simple loneliness, it had taken everything in him to turn away from her.

He pulled into his parking spot and headed toward

his townhouse, but when he dug in his pocket for the door key, he couldn't find it. He checked his other pockets, then retraced his steps to his car, thinking he might have dropped the key. But it was gone. Had he left it at Shelby's hotel room? Frustrated, he grabbed the door knob, wondering if he could force the door open. To his surprise, it turned easily in his hand.

Goose bumps rose along his arm as he stared into the front room. "Hello?" he called, then felt foolish. If someone was inside, were they really going to answer him?

He reached inside and flipped on the light. The room looked undisturbed. Exactly as he left it. He stepped inside. Nothing was out of place. Had he simply forgotten to lock the door when he left for work this morning? He had never done that before, but he had a lot on his mind right now. He went to the bedroom and took his wallet from his pocket and set it on the dresser and checked again for the house key. No, it definitely wasn't in any of his pockets.

He started to unbutton his shirt and turned toward the bathroom and froze. He stared at the small stuffed bear nestled between the pillows at the head of his bed. The kind of thing someone might buy for a child. What was it doing here?

Frowning, he moved closer. The bear, about ten inches tall, stared back at him with amber glass eyes. Was this someone's idea of a joke? Angry now, he leaned forward and snatched up the bear. The head lolled to one side, stuffing spilling from the neck opening. Zach stared, cold all over. Someone had sliced through the neck so that the bear's head hung by a thread.

Chapter Eleven

Shelby reread the last entry in Camille's online journal, trying to find some clue she had missed before about Camille's intentions. But the brief paragraph of an unspecified day's activities was innocuous. *Ran three miles this morning, rewarded myself with an iced mocha. Flirted with Dave, but neither of us is serious about it. Sasha was late again. Sushi for dinner, third time this week. I might be addicted!*

Had she written about such mundane matters to throw Shelby and others like her off the track? There was nothing in the entry about threats or being followed or any suspicion that she might be in danger. That led Shelby to believe that whoever had killed Camille must have picked up her trail after she left her new life in Maryland. Had the Chalk brothers sent someone to watch for any activity near Zach or her parents? Or had they discovered her new identity and merely waited until she was alone and unprotected to strike?

Her phone rang, and she grabbed it up and stared at the screen. "Zach?" She glanced at the clock beside the bed. He had left the motel thirty minutes ago.

He cleared his throat. "Did I happen to leave my house

key in your room?" he asked. "I got home and can't find it."

"I haven't seen it. Let me look." Still holding the phone, she stood and scanned the carpet between the bed and the door, then looked all around the furniture. "I don't see it," she said. "Do you think it could be at Mo's?"

"Maybe."

Something in his voice alarmed her. "Is everything okay? You sound…upset."

A long silence. "Zach?"

"The thing is, when I tried the door, it was unlocked," he said. "I never forget to lock the door."

"Is everything inside okay? Do you want me to come over?"

"Everything is okay. Except…"

That silence again. It felt weighted. And wrong. "Zach, what is it?"

"Someone's been here," he said. "They left a stuffed animal on my bed. A bear. And, well, its head's been cut almost off."

Her stomach dipped, then rose. "Don't touch anything. I'm on my way over."

She hung up before he could protest that he didn't need her to come over. She shut down Camille's laptop and locked it in her suitcase and took it with her when she left the room. She locked the case in the trunk, then drove to Zach's, heart racing, even as she forced herself to stay only a few miles over the speed limit. Zach was all right. Whoever had done this thing hadn't hurt him.

Yet.

She parked beside Zach's truck and scanned the parking lot. No one was visible this time of night, and nothing looked out of place. She slid out of the driver's seat and closed the door softly behind her, not locking it in case she needed to leave suddenly, perhaps with Zach in tow. Then she walked to Zach's door, checking all around her for anything suspicious.

The door itself looked undisturbed. No sign of forced entry. She rang the bell, and within seconds, the door opened. "I'm okay," Zach said before she could speak. "I'm just a little confused."

"Show me," she said.

She followed him into the townhouse, through the living room and down a short hall to the bedroom. Her first impression was of a comfortable room with a king-size bed, a dresser and a bedside table. She focused on the object in the middle of the comforter. A brown stuffed bear, head lolling to one side. It was just a child's toy, but the sight of it, disfigured that way, made her sick to her stomach. "That would freak anyone out," she told Zach, assuming an attitude of calm she didn't really feel. "Where was it, exactly, when you found it?"

"Sitting up between the two pillows at the head of the bed." He gestured toward the pillows. "I picked it up, and the head almost fell off."

"And you're sure the bear wasn't here before?"

He let out a hoarse laugh. "I'm a little old to sleep with a teddy bear."

She shook her head. "Have you seen it—or one like it—before?"

"No."

She pulled out her phone.

"Who are you calling?" His voice rose with alarm.

"The sheriff's department."

"No!" He held out his hands. "I'm okay. Nothing happened. It's just a sick joke."

"You said you lost your house key, right?"

"Yeah."

"And you haven't found it?"

"No. But I probably dropped it—"

"Whoever got in here did it with your key," she said. "That means they took it from you. Who could have done that?"

"No one. The key was in my pocket. I would have noticed if someone had tried to take it."

"Not if the person was good at picking pockets." She studied him. "What about Janie? She was sitting very close to you when I saw you two together at Mo's."

He paled. "When I left, she hugged me."

"She could have taken the key then."

"But why would she? And why do this?"

"I don't know. But we need to find out. The sheriff can help with that."

She made the call. The dispatcher agreed to send a deputy. That settled, she took Zach into the kitchen and got a glass of water for him and one for herself. "Who else was close enough to you today to pick your pocket?" she asked.

"I don't know. Eldon and I climbed together this afternoon. But he wouldn't do something like this."

She could have argued that anyone might do something terrible with the right motivation, but didn't bother. "Anyone else?"

"There was this guy, Todd. We met him in Caspar Canyon, and he tried to help me with my gear. We had a beer with him at Mo's before Janie showed up."

"Is Todd another friend?"

"No. He wrecked an ATV in the high country last week, and Search and Rescue responded to the call."

"So you don't really know anything about him."

"No." He looked miserable.

The doorbell summoned them, and Zach ushered in a sheriff's deputy. "Deputy Declan Owen," he introduced himself. "I understand you had a break-in. What happened?"

Zach explained about losing his key and finding the door open, then showed Deputy Owen the mutilated bear. "Nothing else was disturbed," he said. "It's really strange. And unsettling."

"I noticed the front door didn't look forced," Owen said. "Is there any other way for someone to get in?"

"I didn't think of that." Zach looked to Shelby.

"We should check," she said, wishing she had thought of that before.

They followed Owen through the townhouse, but the back door and all the windows were still secure. "I think someone stole Zach's key and used it to get in," Shelby said.

"Any idea who?" Owen asked Zach.

"I had a couple of strangers approach me this afternoon," Zach said. "Both people I had helped on Search and Rescue calls. I guess one of them might have taken the key, though I don't know why."

Owen wrote down the information on Todd and Janie, then bagged the bear as evidence. "Any idea who might want to frighten you?" he asked Zach.

Zach shook his head. "No."

"Zach's sister was in witness security after she testified

against Charlie and Christopher Chalk in Houston," Shelby said. "Her murderer may have worked for the Chalks. There's the possibility they're targeting Zach now."

"I don't believe it," Zach said. "They don't have any reason to go after me."

"I used to work for the Marshals Service," Owen said. "I know about your sister's case. I'm sorry for your loss."

"Did you know Camille?" Zach asked.

"I met her once, before she was relocated. She had a good reputation in the office—smart and just a really nice person."

Zach nodded. "That was Camille."

"Why did you leave the Marshals Service?" Shelby asked.

"This is a better fit for me," he said. He nodded to Zach. "We'll be in touch. Call us right away if anything else happens that seems off or threatening."

He left. Zach dropped onto the sofa and rested his elbows on his knees. He looked exhausted. "I'll need to change the locks tomorrow," he said.

Shelby sat beside him. "You shouldn't stay here tonight."

"I'll be okay." He glanced to the door. "I'll wedge a chair under the door knob or something."

"If you have a pillow and some blankets, I'll make up a bed here on the sofa," she said.

He straightened. "You don't have to do that."

"I'm not going to leave you alone."

"It was just a stuffed bear," he said. "Sick, but…"

"It was a threat," she said. "Or a warning."

"You really think the Chalk brothers sent someone after me? Why?"

"Maybe killing Camille wasn't enough for them," she said. "Maybe they want to take out her whole family."

He stood. "My parents!"

She put a hand on his arm. "While you and Deputy Owen were in the bedroom, I called my office, and they're sending someone to watch over your parents. I told them I'd look after you."

He sat again. "This is unreal. You really think I'm in danger?"

"You said Janie was at the campground the day Camille was murdered. She has long blond hair."

"Wait. I thought a man killed Camille."

"A tall, thin figure dressed in a hooded raincoat and jeans was seen leaving her campsite. How tall is Janie?"

"Tall," he said. "Almost six feet." He looked stunned. "You really think she murdered Camille?"

"I don't know. What about Todd? What does he look like?"

"He's tall, too. And thin. And he has blond hair." Zach looked as if he might be sick.

"Was he at the campground that day?"

"I don't remember seeing him. But there were a lot of people there. And everyone was wet and bundled up in coats and rain gear."

"I'll work with the sheriff's department to find out where both of them were after they left you yesterday," she said. "In the meantime, I'll stay here tonight."

He stiffened, and she knew he wanted to protest that he could look after himself, but the memory of that almost beheaded bear must have stopped him. "I'll find you some bedding," he said and left the room.

When he was gone, Shelby took out her pistol and

laid it on the coffee table, within easy reach of the sofa. She didn't believe what had happened here tonight was a harmless prank or a sick joke. The person who left that bear wanted to frighten Zach. Fear had a way of wearing people down. Of making them more vulnerable. But she wasn't going to let them get close enough to Zach to harm him. She had failed Camille. She wouldn't fail Zach.

ZACH DIDN'T SLEEP that night. Every time he closed his eyes, he saw that mutilated bear and heard Shelby telling him the Chalk brothers might have decided to come after him. Because they hated Camille so much?

Or because they knew he hadn't told everything he had seen that night in front of the Britannia Pub?

He tossed and turned, then listened as Shelby moved around in the front room. He thought about going out to talk to her. Or to do more than talk. He hadn't forgotten the brief physical connection they had shared in her motel room earlier that evening. How wonderful would it be to focus on exploring that instead of being afraid? To escape for a while in a different kind of emotion?

But that wouldn't be a good idea. And Shelby didn't strike him as the type to get distracted when she had a job to do. So he turned over again and stayed in bed, finally slipping into a troubled sleep full of swirling waters, a blond figure running away from him and a real bear that roared at him from the underbrush.

He went through the next day on autopilot, half expecting his coworkers to ask what was wrong. But everyone was busy in the run-up to the opening of a new mine shaft, and no one questioned the dark circles beneath his eyes or his distracted air.

At four o'clock, Deputy Owen called. "Could you stop by the sheriff's office when you get off work?" he asked.

"Sure. Did you find something?"

"We just have a few more questions to ask you."

Shelby was waiting in the room with Sheriff Walker and Deputy Owen when the office manager, Adelaide Kinkaid, escorted Zach inside a little over an hour later. "Thanks for stopping by," Sheriff Walker said. He nodded to the lone empty chair. "Sit down."

He sat and glanced at Shelby, who looked at him in a way that was probably meant to be reassuring, but only made him brace himself for worse news. "What have you found out about the break-in at my place last night?" he asked.

"None of your neighbors saw anyone suspicious," the sheriff said. "But that's not too surprising, if someone with a key walked up and opened the door and went inside. Most people wouldn't look twice. And the way the townhomes are arranged, your front door faces the street. None of your neighbors could see it from inside their homes."

"Did you talk to Todd or Janie?" he asked.

"Without a last name, we're having trouble locating Janie," the sheriff said. "You say she was at the campground the day Search and Rescue helped evacuate flooded campers?"

"Yes. She came up and hugged me and thanked me for helping out."

"And later at Mo's, she thanked you again?"

"Yes." He frowned.

"You don't remember a last name?" Deputy Owen asked.

"I'm sure she never said. You could ask Eldon Ramsey. He was there, too. And he saw her at the campground."

The sheriff made a note. "What else do you know about her?"

"She said she was camping with friends, but that they left to go to Moab while she stayed in town a few more days."

"What was your impression of her?"

"If you mean, did I think she was the type to steal my key and leave a slashed-up stuffed animal in my townhouse, I sure didn't think that."

"Special Agent Dryden tells us Janie was coming on pretty strong at Mo's."

He didn't look at Shelby, and his cheeks felt hot. "She was flirting."

"There was no one named Janie, and no one who matched that description among the campers we interviewed about your sister," Walker said.

"But I thought you talked to everyone?" Zach asked.

"We were able to match the names of the people we did interview with every occupied site," Walker said.

"Maybe she didn't register," Zach said. "It happens. People occupy a site but don't pay. It's all on the honor system."

"Maybe. Or maybe she wasn't camping there at all." The sheriff glanced at his notes. "We did interview Todd Arniston. Do you remember seeing him at the campground that day?"

"No! He was there? He never said."

"We have a statement from him. But he says he never saw your sister or anyone suspicious."

"I went back out to the campground afterward," Zach said. "It had reopened, but I didn't see Todd there."

"He's moved into town. He's staying at the Nugget Inn. But he was out when a deputy stopped by. The deputy left a card, asking Mr. Arniston to call us."

"If the threat left at your townhouse does have any connection to the Chalk brothers, it might not be a bad idea for you to leave town for a few days," Walker said.

"I can't just leave," he said. "I have a job, and Search and Rescue commitments. And my parents. I can't abandon them."

"I received confirmation this morning that the FBI has a protection detail with your parents," Shelby said.

"Have they been threatened, too?" He needed to call them. He should have called last night, but he hadn't wanted to upset them.

"No. And we haven't told them anything about what happened to you," she said. "They think we're being extra cautious in the aftermath of Camille's death."

He nodded. That was alarming enough, but it was a story his parents would accept. Like him, they would find it difficult to believe they were in any real danger. Not after so much time had passed. Even in the run-up to the trial, when Shelby and her potential testimony had filled the news, Zach and his parents had never felt threatened. All of the focus was on Shelby. As horrible as her death had been, knowing she was gone had made them all believe the Chalk brothers would forget about them.

"I need to stay here," he said. "I'll be careful, but I can't run away."

Shelby pressed her lips together, and he wondered

if she was biting her tongue, too, to keep from arguing with him. Her eyes telegraphed her disagreement with this decision, but she apparently knew him well enough now—or realized he was enough like Camille in this regard—that she didn't waste her words.

Zach stood. "Can I go now?"

Sheriff Walker nodded.

Zach left, Shelby on his heels. "You don't have to babysit me," he said. "I got the locks changed, and I promise to dial 911 if anything at all unusual happens."

"By then it could be too late."

"Look, if Janie or Todd really wanted me dead, wouldn't they have killed me by now? They've had plenty of opportunities. You don't think Camille had days and days of warnings, do you?"

She probably wouldn't appreciate it if he told her she looked cute when she frowned like that. Something about her intensity really got to him. "You shouldn't be alone," she said.

"You can't stay with me," he said.

"Why not?"

"You're too distracting." He met and held her gaze. The faintest blush of pink colored her cheeks.

"I… I'm sure we can get past that," she stammered.

Did he really want to "get past" his feelings for her? He shook his head. "I'll stay in touch."

She let him walk away, though he felt the effort it took. Once he was in his truck, he looked back. She was still frowning at him, lips pressed tightly together. What did it say about him that in spite of everything else, all he wanted to do was kiss her?

Chapter Twelve

"There's been a new development." Shelby sat up straight and kept her expression neutral, just as if she was seated across from Special Agent in Charge Lester, instead of speaking to him on the phone. "A threat has been made against Camille Gregory's brother, and I've identified two suspects in her murder. I need to stay in Eagle Mountain a little longer."

"Who are the suspects?" Lester asked.

"A man calling himself Todd Arniston and a woman named Janie. Both names could be aliases. They were known to be in the same area as Camille at the time of her murder, and they have both shown an unusual interest in Zach Gregory. His townhouse was broken into the other night after his house key was taken, and both of them had the opportunity to take the key."

"Have the local authorities brought them in for questioning?"

"After the break-in at Zach's, they've disappeared, though I believe they are still in the area." She had no proof of this, merely a strong hunch.

"How was Gregory threatened?"

She explained about the mutilated bear. "Camille

often referred to her brother as a 'bear of a man' or a 'teddy bear of a man,'" she added.

"This doesn't sound like the Chalk brothers," Lester said. "They don't play games with the people they kill. They assassinate them, and they don't leave evidence behind."

"If Todd or Janie are working for the Chalk brothers, they haven't shown up on our radar before," she admitted. "But Camille definitely believed her brother was in danger. I think that's why she came to Eagle Mountain."

"If she believed that, she should have shared her fears with the Marshals Service and the FBI and allowed us to investigate," Lester said.

"Yes, sir." Shelby thought she knew why Camille hadn't done so. She hadn't trusted law enforcement to act on her suspicions. Or she hadn't believed they would act in time. Testimony at the Chalk brothers trial had shown that the FBI was aware of the threat to Judge Hennessey weeks before he was murdered, and they had failed to act. Camille hadn't wanted to take a chance that her brother would meet the same fate.

"We have the DNA results on the hair you sent from Camille's campsite," Lester said. "There's no match in any database we've consulted."

"So this could be someone the Chalks haven't used before."

"Or someone unrelated to the Chalk brothers. Camille was a single woman, camping alone. She could have been killed by someone random who saw her and decided to kill her, or because she refused someone's advances, or because they wanted her campsite. As much as we'd like to prove the Chalk brothers are guilty of some crime, not everything necessarily relates back to them."

"Yes, sir. But we need to prove that before we move on. I'd like to stay a little longer and continue to look for Todd and Janie. Questioning them might clear up everything."

"All right. We'll take it day by day."

She ended the call and stood. She might not have much time left in town, so she needed to get to work.

She started at the front desk of the Ranch Motel. No registration for anyone who fit Janie's description. She moved on to the Nugget Inn, a sprawling new property in the center of town. The sheriff's department had said Arniston was registered here, but the clerk confirmed that he had checked out the previous afternoon.

"Do you have a woman named Janie registered here?" she asked.

"Do you have a last name?" the clerk, a middle-aged woman with short, tightly curled hair, looked suspicious of this snooping.

"I don't." Shelby pulled out her credentials and watched the woman's eyes widen as she took in the official Federal Bureau of Investigation logo. "But I'd like to speak to her if she's here."

The woman shook her head. "We don't have anyone named Janie here."

"She's in her late twenties to early thirties, blond hair and very tall—almost six feet."

"She sounds like a model," the clerk said.

She had looked like one, too. "Do you have anyone who fits that description staying here?" Shelby asked.

"No. I'm sure I'd remember someone like that."

"Are there any other motels or hotels in town? Other than this one and the Ranch Motel?"

"There's the Alpiner—that's a bed-and-breakfast inn. And there are a lot of private rentals."

A pleasant older woman at the Alpiner confirmed that neither Janie nor Todd was staying with them. Shelby left the inn and sat in her car, trying to decide what to do next. She phoned Zach. He answered on the fourth ring, the sound of heavy equipment in the background. "Hello?"

"It's me, Shelby," she said. "How are you doing?"

"I'm at work. And I'm kind of busy."

He sounded annoyed. He was probably still upset with her. Because she was being overprotective? Or because she distracted him? She had wanted him to explain exactly how she distracted him, but was a little afraid of the answer. Maybe she had only imagined that he had wanted to kiss her that night in her motel room. And maybe she was the only one who tossed and turned later that same night at his townhouse, aware of him occupying the bed in the next room. He was a good-looking man, and through his sister she had come to know him better and care about him. Her attraction to him was natural, not unprofessional. But acting on it would be, and it would be downright embarrassing if she had misjudged his feelings. Maybe she distracted him because she reminded him of what had happened to his sister, or the way that the FBI and Witness Security had inadvertently ruined his family's lives.

Too bad. She was going to look out for him whether he thought he needed her or not. For one thing, if Camille's killer was hanging around intending to take out Zach,

Shelby's best chance of catching the murderer might be to intercept him on the way to Zach. Two, she owed it to Camille to protect what was left of her family. There were other agents watching Zach's parents, but she was all he had. "What are you doing after work?" she asked.

"Going back to my place."

"I'll come over."

"You don't have to do that."

"I don't have to stay, but I want to talk to you."

She wasn't sure if the silence that followed was because he was debating the question or due to an interruption. "I'll bring pizza," she added.

"All right," he said. "You can come over around six. And I like pepperoni and sausage. No mushrooms."

He ended the call before she could say anything else. She smiled. Zach might be put out with her, but he wasn't shutting her out altogether. She counted that a small victory, at least.

ZACH REMINDED HIMSELF again that inviting Shelby over was probably a bad idea, but he hadn't been able to say no. Around her, he didn't have to pretend nothing was wrong. No one at work or among his friends knew about his stolen house key and the sinister stuffed bear. And unlike the FBI agents he had dealt with before and after the Chalk brothers trial, he thought Shelby would tell him if she learned anything about Camille's murderer or whoever had threatened him.

But when he opened his door and found her standing there in cropped jeans and a sleeveless black top that showed off toned arms, her hair loose about her shoulders, he questioned the wisdom of letting her inside. She didn't look like an FBI agent right now. She looked like a woman he wanted to date.

"Let me in before this pizza gets cold," she said, hefting the large pizza box she carried in both hands.

"Sure." He looked away as she brushed past him, but her floral perfume teased him over the scent of pepperoni.

He moved past her. "Come on into the kitchen."

She followed him, and he took plates and glasses from the cabinet. He didn't ask what she was doing here. "What would you like to drink?" he asked. "I've got beer and water."

"Water is fine."

"Are you saying that because you're on duty?"

"I'm saying it because I don't really like beer. But you go ahead."

He took a pale ale from the refrigerator and filled a glass with ice and water for her. She opened the pizza box. He studied the pizza before him. "Are those mushrooms?" he asked.

"Only on half the pizza. Your half doesn't have any."

"You didn't think I could eat more than half?"

"If you do, you'll have to pick off the mushrooms." She popped a bite of the topping in question into her mouth. "I love them."

He kind of liked that she didn't back down or try to cater to him. Or pretend that she didn't like mushrooms either—he had encountered women like that before, who tried too hard to please. Shelby clearly wasn't trying to please him at all. How perverse was it that it made him like her more?

They sat and began to eat. For a while, neither of

them spoke. Hunger sated, he began to feel a little better. "Any new developments?" he asked.

"Todd checked out of his hotel yesterday afternoon. No one seems to have seen or heard of Janie."

"Do you think they've left town?"

"I don't know. But I'm operating on the assumption that they haven't." She plucked a mushroom from her slice of pizza and popped it into her mouth. She wasn't wearing any lipstick that he could tell, but her lips were a natural pink. They looked soft.

At the thought, he looked away again. "If they have left," he said, "it blows away your theory that I'm in danger."

"Maybe not in danger from them. But whoever killed Camille is still out there."

Right. Sobering thought. "Have you found out anything more?"

"No. Has anything else happened to raise your suspicions? Have you seen anyone following you? Have you received any threats you haven't told me about?"

The way she fired the questions reminded him that she was a law enforcement officer with a job to do. Not his friend, or date. "No. Honest."

"I believe you."

They finished eating. She slid the last piece of pizza toward him. "You can have this one. I picked all the fungi off it for you."

The way she said it, with a sneer of sarcasm, made him laugh out loud. He ate the pizza, then stood to carry the box to the trash. "Thanks for dinner," he said.

She rose also.

"You said you wanted to talk to me," he said.

"Let's go into the other room."

They moved to the living room, and he settled on the sofa, her in a chair across from him, hands on her knees. "The results of the DNA test on the hair we found at Camille's campsite didn't find a match in our database," she said. "That doesn't mean the hair doesn't belong to her killer, only that the killer might not be someone known to us."

"Someone associated with the Chalk brothers, you mean?"

"They have a big organization. We have files on most of the principals, but it's always possible they've brought in someone new. It's also possible that Camille's killing has nothing to do with the Chalk brothers. And it's possible that the threat to you isn't connected to Camille."

He stared. "Are you saying my sister dies and someone steals my key and plants a mutilated stuffed animal in my bed and those are just two random things? Bad luck?"

"I'm saying I don't know." She moved to the edge of the chair. "Who knew that Camille nicknamed you after a bear?"

"I don't know. I guess anyone who knew her. It wasn't a secret."

"She told me you were a bear of a man and a big teddy bear. Did she tell other people that?"

"Maybe. I don't know."

"Does anyone in Eagle Mountain know about it?"

He shook his head. "No. I never talk about Camille with people." Only with Shelby. He looked away, trying to control his emotions. "I miss her," he said. "I thought maybe after a while I wouldn't miss her so much, but

I still do." He didn't think of calling her every day, the way he had for a while, but there was still an emptiness inside his chest when he thought of her.

"I do, too." Her eyes met his, and he saw his own pain reflected there.

He couldn't keep looking at her this way. It made him too unsettled, wanting things he shouldn't. He stood, and she rose also. "Was she really happy there, in Maryland?" he asked.

"I think so. I mean, none of us are happy all the time, but she had a job she enjoyed and friends, a nice house. I thought she was pretty well settled."

"How did the two of you become friends? I know you said you questioned her about the Chalk brothers, but it sounds like you stayed in touch after that."

"We just really hit it off," Shelby said. "We were about the same age, and she was easy to talk to. She was so smart and thoughtful, and she was a risk-taker. I guess we had that in common."

"I guess you don't get into law enforcement if you're the type who always wants to play it safe." He glanced at her again, and she was looking at him, head tilted to one side, as if she was studying a painting or statue. What was she seeing? Was he Camille's brother to her? A potential witness who could contribute to her case? A guy who had lost his sister, someone she felt sorry for? A man she wanted to know better?

"She talked about you a lot," Shelby said. "She said people underestimated you because you were such a big guy. They sometimes treated you like a dumb jock, when you were really smart."

He shook his head. What she said wasn't a lie, but it wasn't like he was a genius or anything.

"She said you were really funny, too, with this dry sense of humor and a deadpan delivery. She told me so many stories. I felt like I knew you even before I met you."

Camille could have told her some stories, all right. "She probably told you all my most embarrassing moments."

"Only the endearing ones. She never told me anything bad."

"I let her take all the heat from the Chalk brothers," he said. "I never admitted I was waiting for her that night at the pub."

"You did it for your parents. And for her."

"Maybe. But it was also easier not to get involved. When I saw what the prosecution put her through on the stand, I was glad that wasn't me up there being cross-examined."

"I read the trial transcripts," Shelby said. "She did a great job."

"She did. And then afterward..." The familiar vise squeezed his chest. He would never forget the FBI agent telling them that Camille was dead. That moment still replayed itself in his nightmares. His sister had vanished from his life at that moment, even if her real death had occurred four years later.

Shelby rose and put her hand on his arm. She had small hands, and her touch was delicate, but he felt the heat of her seeping into him. "I'm sorry," she said. "I'm sorry we put you through that pain. Not once, but twice."

He shrugged. "Camille agreed to it." Maybe later he

would wrestle more with that idea—that Camille had played a part in deceiving him and his parents. She had always thought she knew what was best, but had she, really?

"She agreed," Shelby said, "but I don't believe it was easy for her. She wanted to protect you all."

"And it cost her everything."

He met her gaze again, and she moved closer, until they were almost touching. Her hand was still on his arm, and she brought her other hand up to grip the other arm, as if she might shake him. Maybe she was going to tell him to snap out of it, to quit moping and get on with his life. Other people had said as much.

But instead of scolding him, she pulled him close and laid her head on his chest. He slid his arms around her and returned the embrace, the intensity of the moment almost overwhelming—sadness and regret and a rush of desire a confusing cocktail surging through him. The perfume of her hair, gently floral, surrounded him, and her breasts, soft and rounded, pressed against him. He slid his hand along her spine, tracing the fine bones, down to the dip above the curve of her backside. She must be feeling how much he wanted her, and he expected her to pull away at any moment.

Instead, she tilted her head to look up at him again, her eyes half closed, her lips soft and parted in invitation.

He kissed her, pausing when his lips met hers, giving her time to pull away. Instead, she returned the caress and brought one hand up to cradle the back of his neck, urging him closer still.

SHELBY HAD WANTED this from the first day she had met Zach Gregory. She had told herself her desire was inappropriate and would never be returned. She was used to the men she encountered on the job seeing her as an agent first and a woman second. That was how she wanted to be seen 99 percent of the time.

But Zach... Zach wasn't just any man. Everything Camille had told her had built up the image of this strong, thoughtful, sexy man. The kind of man she had longed for in her life. And then she had met him in person, and he had turned out to be so much more.

He deepened the kiss, and she arched her body to his. He shaped his hands to her backside and slid one thigh between her legs, tucking her in closer still, and she gasped at the sensation. He slid his tongue into her opened mouth, and she gave up all pretense of holding back, sliding her hands beneath his shirt to caress his muscled back.

Two sharp, loud reports that sounded as if they came from right outside the door made them freeze. Heart hammering hard in her chest, she pushed away from him. "That sounded like gunfire," she said. Hours spent at the firing range had drilled that particular percussive echo into her brain. She raced to the kitchen and retrieved her own weapon from her purse, then moved to the door, Zach right behind her.

"Maybe it's just a car backfiring," he said, his last words almost drowned out by the piercing squeal of brakes and the growl of tires on gravel.

Shelby wrenched open the door and peered out in time to see the red glow of disappearing headlights. The silence that followed fell heavy as a blanket. "I don't see anyone," Zach said. He stood over her, also looking out the door.

She waited another long minute, then opened the door a little wider. Zach's neighbor emerged from his door. "What was that?" he asked when he saw the two of them looking out.

Shelby tucked the gun in the back of her jeans and pulled her shirt down over it. "I don't know," she said. "Did you see anyone?"

The neighbor shook his head. "Maybe it was a car backfiring."

Still wary, Shelby stepped outside, but Zach pushed past her. "Your car," he said, and pointed at the rental Shelby had picked up in Junction. The sedan leaned sharply to one side. She followed Zach over to the vehicle and looked down at the flat tires on the passenger side. The tread on the nearest tire had clearly been shredded by the impact of a bullet.

The neighbor had followed them out. The young, stocky man, dressed in gray joggers and a T-shirt that didn't quite cover his belly, let out a low whistle. "Someone doesn't like you," he said.

Shelby suppressed a shudder. She was used to people not liking her, or at least not liking the job she had to do. But maybe this attack wasn't really about her. Maybe whoever had done this had known she was inside with Zach, and he was the real target.

Chapter Thirteen

For the second time in as many nights, Zach stood in the parking lot in front of his townhouse with a sheriff's deputy. Shelby was talking to the wrecker driver who had come to tow her rental car to his shop, where he had promised he would replace her destroyed tires in the morning.

"Do you think the same person who shot out her tires broke into my townhouse last night?" Zach asked.

Deputy Owen turned from his contemplation of the car to meet Zach's gaze. "I don't know," he said. "Do you?"

"Maybe whoever did this thought that was my car." He looked past her to his truck, parked just a few spaces down.

"Maybe," Owen said. "Or maybe they knew the car belonged to an FBI agent and were making some kind of statement."

Zach nodded. In the almost two weeks Shelby had been in Eagle Mountain, plenty of people would have passed on the news that an FBI agent was staying at the Ranch Motel. They probably even knew she was investigating the murder of a woman at the Forest Service campground. A few of them might even have connected Zach to the woman. Everyone on Search and

Rescue knew that last fact, and one or more of them might have talked.

"What was Agent Dryden doing here tonight?" Owen asked.

Besides kissing me senseless? Zach struggled to turn his thoughts toward a safer answer. "She had some more questions about what happened here last night," he said.

Shelby stood back as the wrecker hooked on to her car then slowly winched it onto the flatbed. She waved as the wrecker drove away, then rejoined Zach and Deputy Owen. "He thinks he has the right tires in stock and can get them on first thing in the morning," she said.

"That's good." Though he felt stupid as soon as the words were out of his mouth. Nothing about this situation was good.

She turned to the deputies. "Can I see those bullets you recovered?"

Owen took a small bag from the left breast pocket of his uniform shirt and passed it to her. She studied the two misshapen slugs in the bag. "Twenty-two long rifle," she said.

"Common as dirt," Owen said. "We'll check for prints, but I doubt we'll find anything." He returned the bag to his pocket. "Have you made any enemies lately, Agent Dryden?"

She shook her head. "I don't think this was about me."

All eyes focused on Zach. He held up both hands. "I don't know what's going on," he said. "I haven't done anything to anyone."

"We can give you a ride to the motel," Deputy Owen said.

"I'll take her," Zach said before Shelby could answer.

"I'll go with Zach," she said. "But thank you."

They waited until Deputy Owen had left before they went back inside the townhouse. The closeness of moments before had vanished, replaced by tension like a thick fog between them. Shelby collected her purse and slung it over her shoulder. "I apologize for my unprofessional behavior," she said, looking not at Zach, but at the space where only moments before they had clung to each other.

"I don't know. I thought you kissed pretty good for an amateur."

She glared at him. So much for trying to lighten the moment. "I don't think you did anything wrong," he said. He moved in closer to embrace her, but she sidestepped the move.

"I doubt my supervisors would agree."

"What say do they have over your personal life?"

"You're part of a case I'm working on."

"I'm not a witness or a victim," he said. "And I'm not a criminal." He didn't know why he was arguing with her. He wasn't in the habit of trying to persuade women who didn't want to be with him. Except that her reluctance didn't seem to be about him at all, but about some ideal she was holding herself to, or thought her bosses were holding her to. And that kiss had been pretty spectacular. He was reluctant to let go of the chance to repeat it, and take it further.

"We should go," she said, and turned her back on him and walked to the door.

He debated not going after her. She wasn't going to get very far without him. Then again, he wouldn't put it past her to walk all the way back to town. It wasn't an impossible distance, but the walk probably wouldn't endear her to him. So he pulled out his keys and followed her out.

He drove toward town but was reluctant to end the night this way. And he didn't necessarily want to be alone with his thoughts, either. He told himself having his apartment broken into and Shelby's tires shot out were only nuisances that should be ignored. No one had been hurt. But he couldn't make himself believe it. Sure, no one had been hurt *yet*. Tonight, some unknown assailant had shot out Shelby's tires. How much of a stretch was it for them to shoot a person instead of a car?

He smoothed his hands down the steering wheel. "I'm too wired to sleep," he said. "Do you want to get some coffee?"

She shifted in her seat. "Where?"

"The only place is the gas station." He glanced at her. Streetlights bathed half her face in a golden glow. "I don't promise it's good coffee."

"All right."

He drove to the station at the intersection leading into town and left the engine running while he ran inside and bought two cups of coffee from the machine at the back of the store. He grabbed a handful of sugar and creamer packets, paid, returned to the car and handed her everything. "Hold this until I find a place we can sit and talk."

He ended up parking on the street a block from the motel. It was after ten, and all the businesses in this part of town were closed, the sidewalks empty. The only streetlight was at the end of the block, so he and Shelby sat in deep shadow. He sipped his coffee and was reminded of the night he had sat on that Houston street, waiting for Camille to emerge from Britannia Pub.

"What are you thinking?" Shelby asked.

He could have lied and said he was thinking about her and the kiss they had shared. Or he might have tried to make a joke about how small towns really did roll up the sidewalks after dark. Instead, he opted for the truth. "I'm thinking about that night at the Britannia. The night Judge Hennessey was shot."

"Tell me about it," she said.

So many times over the years he had relived that evening, running through the events minute by minute, by turns berating himself for keeping silent and telling himself he had no choice. The words to describe what had happened ought to come easily, but he found himself faltering.

"Like you said, Camille's car was in the shop," he said. "She planned to ride the bus home, but I was free and decided to surprise her by picking her up. I parked across the street and waited for her."

"Could you see the pub from where you were parked?" Shelby asked.

"I could see the side of the building and the door that opened onto the alley that Camille would come out of. I couldn't see the front door or into the restaurant."

"Okay. Go on. I didn't mean to interrupt."

"Camille came out and said good-night to her co-workers. They left and she locked up, then started walking toward the bus stop. I pulled alongside her and said hello, and she got in the truck, and I drove away. But we hadn't gone very far before she remembered she had left her wallet behind. I circled back, parked in the same spot and she went back into the restaurant. I noticed she was taking a while, but thought maybe the wallet wasn't where she thought she had left it and she was looking around. Then I heard a loud popping—like firecrackers or a car backfiring. I thought that was what it was—someone shooting off firecrackers on the next street over. Then Camille came running out, dove into the truck and told me to get out of there. I drove away, and she told me what had happened—that Judge Hennessey had been killed, and the Chalk brothers did it. She had me drive her to the police station. She said she would go in and tell them what she had seen and I should go home and not tell anyone I had been there."

He set the half-full cup of bitter coffee in the cup holder and swiveled toward her. "I didn't want to leave her," he said. "I tried to convince her that we should go to the police together, but the suggestion made her frantic. She insisted there was no reason for me to risk coming to the Chalk brothers' attention. She had all the information the police would need. I needed to go home and be with our parents."

"So that's what you did."

He slid down in the seat. "That's what I did. The next day, police arrested the Chalk brothers, Camille went into protective custody and FBI agents showed up at my apartment and my parents' house."

"And you never said anything about being there that night?"

He blew out a breath. "Maybe I should have, but no one ever asked. Camille had it all under control. All the focus was on her, and I guess everyone believed her when she said she was at the restaurant by herself."

"But you were there," Shelby said. Clearly, she wasn't going to cut him any slack.

"Yes. I told you I was in my truck, parked across the street. I wasn't inside the restaurant."

"You heard the gunshot."

"Yes. Though I didn't know it was a gunshot."

She leaned toward him. "How many gunshots?"

"Two. Pop-pop." The sound had jolted him, but it hadn't frightened him. "It wasn't that loud, really."

"Did you see anyone near the restaurant before or after those shots?"

He hesitated. Shelby pounced on that hesitation. "What is it?" she demanded. "What did you see?"

"Right after the shots, a man ran into the intersection ahead of where I was parked."

The sharp intake of her breath told him she hadn't expected that. He braced himself for her to berate him for lying to her until now, but all she said was, "How long after?"

"A minute? Maybe a little less."

"Which direction did he run from?"

"From the direction of the restaurant. But I don't know that he came from the restaurant itself. He could have been walking down the street, heard the shots and they frightened him, so he ran."

"What did he look like?" she asked.

He closed his eyes, bringing the image in his memory into focus. "He was young—early twenties, maybe? He had kind of a large nose and a prominent chin. He was wearing dark pants and a white shirt."

"Would you recognize him if you saw him again?"

He had asked himself that question many times. "I don't know. Maybe."

"Did he see you?"

"No. He stopped in the middle of the intersection and looked my way, but I ducked down."

"Why did you do that?"

"I don't know." He shook his head. "I just reacted. I didn't think. When I raised my head again, he was gone."

"And you didn't think what you saw was important enough to mention?" Her voice was sharp, her words cutting.

"It was just a man in the street. I didn't think he had anything to do with the murder. Camille said the Chalk brothers killed the judge."

"That man could have been another potential witness. He could have even been the witness who guaranteed a conviction. The Chalk brothers might have gone free because you didn't say anything."

If she was trying to make him feel worse about his choice, she was wasting her breath. He had told himself all these things over the years. "I get it," he said. "I was a coward. I let my sister take the fall when I might have drawn some of the Chalk brothers' attention away from her. Don't think I'm proud of what happened, because I'm not." He turned the key in the ignition. "I'll take you to the motel."

She put a hand on his arm. "This isn't over," she said. "You have to give a formal statement. We'll get a forensic artist to work with you and come up with a picture of the man you saw. We might still be able to find him."

"He was just some poor kid on the street that night. He probably didn't have anything to do with the judge's murder. And he didn't kill Camille. That's the only death I care about."

"I want to find this man and talk to him."

"What difference is that going to make?" he asked. "The Chalk brothers were acquitted."

"You never know. It might make a difference."

"And then what happens? The Chalk brothers find out who I am, and I have to go into witness protection, like Camille? Are you going to tell my parents I died, too? Because I'm not going to put them through that."

"No one has to know about this," she said. "Even if we find the man you saw, no one has to know unless there's a new trial."

"A trial for what?"

"I don't know. But you have to give your statement."

He checked his mirrors, then pulled into the street and drove down the block to the motel. "I'm not going to talk about this anymore tonight," he said.

He could feel her staring and sensed her wanting to say more, but he kept his gaze forward and his mouth shut until he heard the door of the truck open and the slide of fabric against the upholstery as she got out. "We're not done," she said, just before she slammed the door.

"Yeah, we are," he said softly. She could grill him about what he had seen that night, and he could give all the details to an FBI artist to reconstruct the image of the fleeing man. But none of that would bring back Camille or find the man who had killed her.

None of that would put Shelby back in his arms or have her kissing him again. Kissing him as if she never wanted to stop.

Chapter Fourteen

Zach was at his desk at the mine when he received a text from Eagle Mountain Search and Rescue. Injured hiker Cascade Trail near falls. The choice between continuing to transcribe the most recent assay figures or hiking a beautiful mountain trail to help someone wasn't a difficult one to make. Zach shut down his computer and walked down the hall to his supervisor's office. "I got a page about an injured hiker," he said. "I don't have anything pressing going on right now."

"Go." Devlin Shaw, chief metallurgical engineer, waved toward the door. "And be careful."

Zach wasn't surprised to see Eldon jogging across the parking lot ahead of him. Zach waved and followed Eldon's Jeep out of the lot to Search and Rescue headquarters.

"Danny's stuck at work," Ryan informed them when they, along with Caleb, Anna and Christine, assembled at headquarters. "I talked to Hannah. EMS has been in phone contact with the hiker, a sixty-year-old woman, Lynette Marx. She slipped on loose rock, and it sounds like she broke her ankle. We need to take a wheeled litter up the trail and get her down to the ambulance."

This kind of rescue wasn't as exciting or potentially dangerous as evacuating someone off the side of the mountain, but it still required the team to work together to make sure they had all the equipment they needed to get the patient to medical help safely. "There are some steep, rocky sections on that trail," Eldon said as he and Zach loaded the collapsible litter onto the team's rescue vehicle, dubbed the Beast. "It will take some muscle to get the loaded litter over those."

"Everybody watch your step," Ryan advised as he added a pack with medical supplies to the load. "The last thing we want is to have to evacuate one of you because you broke a bone, too."

Fifteen minutes later, they arrived at the Cascade trailhead to find a waiting ambulance and a handful of onlookers. Most appeared to be fellow hikers, identifiable by their daypacks and hiking boots. But a flash of blond hair made Zach do a double take. The woman had her back to him, but she was tall, and he was almost sure it was Janie. But that couldn't be right. Shelby had said the local deputies hadn't been able to locate her to question her after Zach's apartment was broken into.

"What's she doing here?" Eldon spoke over Zach's shoulder. He was also staring at the woman, who was walking away now. Almost as if she hadn't seen them.

"I don't know." Zach wanted to go after her, but he couldn't leave the team. Instead, he crouched to slide the straps of a pack onto his shoulders, then carefully straightened. One-half of the litter was strapped to Zach's pack. Caleb already had the pack with the other half of the litter, while Eldon would carry the mounting bracket and single wheel that would help them get the loaded litter down the trail. The rest of the team carried braces, splints, helmets and other medical and safety gear.

Hannah Richards, a Rayford County paramedic, waited for them at the trailhead. She would be in charge of the medical assessment and delivering any pain medication the patient might need. Ryan looked back over the assembled group. "All right," he said. "Let's go."

As Zach headed out, he took a last look at the hikers milling about the parking area. No sign of the blonde. Maybe his mind was playing tricks on him. Janie wouldn't have ignored him—although maybe she was upset that he had turned down her advances the other night. And Eldon had thought it was her, too.

He stumbled and Anna put out a hand to steady him. "Thanks," he muttered, and focused on the trail. The hike was a steep one, switchbacking up the side of the mountain on a path that was supposedly once used by mule teams to transport ore from the now defunct Simpson mine. The mine ruins were a popular draw for hikers, as was the view from the top of the trail into a wildflower-filled basin. Zach was soon breathing hard, but keeping up with the others. No one spoke much, focused on moving as quickly as possible toward a woman who was probably in pain.

Lynette Marx was pale but cheerful when they reached her. "I am so glad to see you all," she said as the volunteers surrounded her. She lay on the ground in a stand of aspen trees beside the trail, one foot, stripped of its hiking boot, propped on a fallen tree, her pack beneath her head. A young couple who had been hiking behind her had seen her slip and stopped to help, and the man had run down the trail until he had enough phone signal to call for help. Then he had returned to stay with Lynette and his wife until rescuers arrived.

While Eldon, Caleb and Zach assembled the litter, Hannah assessed Lynette's injuries, administered a painkiller and fitted her with a splint. "That feels better already," Lynette said as they prepared to load her onto the litter. Once she was tucked in securely, the team members arranged themselves around the litter and prepared for the trip down the mountain.

A little over an hour later, they were back at the trailhead, and Lynette was being loaded into the waiting ambulance. A few curious onlookers had gathered, but no tall blonde woman was among them. Zach helped pack up their gear and rode back to headquarters. "Good job, everybody," Ryan said. "It couldn't have gone any smoother."

At headquarters, they unloaded the Beast. Zach checked his watch, then decided to head back to the mine to finish his report. But first, he pulled out his phone.

"Hello?" Shelby answered right away.

"I was just on a Search and Rescue call near Cascade Falls," Zach said. "There was a woman in the crowd who might have been Janie. Her back was to me, so maybe I'm wrong, but Eldon was there, and he thought it was her, too. She moved away before I had a chance to speak to her."

"Did you see where she went?"

"No. I was busy with the rescue and couldn't keep an eye on her."

"Where is Cascade Falls?" she asked.

He gave her directions. "There were a lot of people

there," he said. "It's a popular hiking area. It might not even have been her."

"If you and Eldon both recognized her, it was probably Janie," she said. "I'll see what I can find out."

Zach wondered if he should be more worried. But he couldn't see the overly flirtatious blonde as a real threat, no matter what Shelby said. Janie was just a woman who had a crush on him. Harmless.

Back at work, he realized the break had done him good—the figures weren't quite so boring, and by six he was happy with the job he had done.

He was less happy when he parked by his townhouse and saw a familiar figure waiting by the door to his home. "What are you doing here?" he demanded when Todd Arniston straightened at his approach. Todd wore jeans and a T-shirt and a messenger bag slung over one shoulder.

"I was hoping we could talk," Todd said. "Just the two of us."

Zach stopped several feet away, wary. This guy didn't look like an assassin. Then again, what did an assassin look like? "I'm glad you weren't badly hurt in your accident, and I was happy to help," Zach said, "but I don't think we have anything else to say to each other." He needed to get inside and call Shelby. And maybe the sheriff, too. He tried to move past the other man to unlock his door, but Todd stepped in front of him.

"I want to be straight with you," Todd said. "I'm not just a hapless tourist. I'm a writer. I'm working on a book about the Chalk brothers."

Zach went very still. Was this guy telling the truth? "So you're not just here on vacation?"

Todd's face reddened. "I am, but I'm also here to see you. I've been researching this book ever since the Chalk brothers trial, and I've got lots of great material. I wanted to interview your sister, but she disappeared before I had a chance to talk to her. So I tracked you down to here and thought you could tell me about her. I mean, I really can't tell this story without including Camille."

Zach's new house key bit into his palm where he gripped it so tightly. "Why didn't you tell me you were at the Forest Service campground when it flooded?" he asked. "Were you following Camille? Were you the man someone saw around Camille's campsite the day she was killed?"

Todd's eyes widened. "I didn't know Camille was there! I thought she was dead. Everyone did. I was there camping, like everyone else. I was trying to figure out how to contact you. I didn't even know until later that you were part of the Search and Rescue team. I was too focused on getting out of there safely."

His expression transformed from fear to excitement. "There was a man at her campsite before she died? Seriously? Do the cops think he killed her? What can you tell me about that?" He pulled a pad of paper and a pen from his messenger bag.

"I can't tell you anything." Zach took a step forward, forcing Todd to move out of the way, and inserted the key in the lock.

"You can tell me about Camille," Todd said. "She's such an important part of the story. What she did—testifying against the Chalk brothers—that took a lot of guts. I see her as the real heroine of the story, you know. But I need that personal touch—a glimpse of her personality. You can show me that."

Zach turned away. His memories of Camille were personal and not something he cared to share with a stranger. Talking about her wouldn't bring her back, and doing so wouldn't help put the Chalk brothers behind bars. That was the worst thing about this whole sorry mess—Camille had given up everything, including her life, to try to bring justice to two killers who were never going to pay for their crimes. She could have still been alive, maybe with a partner and children, a career she loved, still with her friends and family. Instead, she was gone, and they had nothing.

"Talk to me, Zach," Todd prompted.

"I don't have anything to say." He shoved open the door. When Todd tried to follow, Zach slammed the door in his face.

Todd pounded on the door. "Let me in," he said. "I just want ten minutes."

"Go away, or I'll call the police."

That shut him up. Zach went into the kitchen and pulled out his phone. "Todd Arniston was here," he told Shelby as soon as she answered. "He says he's writing a book about the Chalk brothers, and he wants to interview me about Camille." He returned to the front window and watched Todd's white sedan pull out of the parking lot. "He's gone now."

"Why didn't you keep him there until the sheriff or I could get there?"

"Because I don't want to talk to the guy. And it's not like he threatened me or anything. Now you know for sure he's still in town, so you should be able to find him. I have to go now."

He sank onto the sofa, his good mood of earlier in the day vanished. Not for the first time, he told himself he never should have driven Camille to the police station the night the judge was killed. He should have taken her home and told her to keep her mouth shut. To stay safe.

Even as he thought this, a smile tugged at his mouth as he imagined Camille's reaction to this ploy. She would have lectured him, probably about justice but also about how no one was going to tell her what to do with her life, especially not her *little* brother. Never mind that Zach was almost a foot taller than her.

Then he should have gone into the police station with her and told his story about seeing a man running down the street near the pub right after the shots were fired.

Again, Camille's reply came to him—her actual words this time. "They don't need what you have to say." Only much later had he realized the subtext behind that message. Camille wanted to be the star of this show. She didn't want to share the spotlight with Zach, whose "evidence" probably didn't mean anything anyway. Camille was the eyewitness. She was the one who mattered.

Zach believed that, too. Shelby talked about police artists and trying to find that running man, but that wasn't going to convict the Chalk brothers. Whoever that guy was, he had simply been in the wrong place at the wrong time. Just like Zach.

The doorbell rang, and he blew out an exasperated breath, then heaved himself off the sofa and stalked to the door. "I told you to leave me alone!" he bellowed, and turned the dead bolt.

Shelby glared up at him. "You didn't say anything about leaving you alone, and even if you did, I wouldn't have listened," she said, and pushed past him into the living room.

"Sorry." He closed the door behind her. "I thought maybe Todd had come back."

"I called the sheriff's department after I talked to you, and they're looking for him. It would help if you could tell us what he was driving."

"A white sedan. Something small. A Chevy, I think. Probably a rental car."

"What did he say to you?"

Zach sat once more. "Apparently the real reason he's been following me around isn't because he's grateful Search and Rescue saved his bacon when he wrecked his ATV on the Jeep trails, but because he wants to interview me about Camille."

"Then why not come right out and ask you to talk to him?"

"Maybe because he knew I'd turn him down flat."

"What else did he say?"

"I asked him if he was the man seen at Camille's campsite before she was killed, and he got pretty excited," Zach said. "He swears he didn't know Camille was at the campground, or even that she was alive. For what it's worth, I believe him."

She sat in the chair across from him. Putting distance between them, he thought. Making sure there was no repeat of the other night. She didn't have to worry. He had gotten the message. No more kissing the fed. "Did you get your tires fixed?" he asked.

"Yes. But we have no idea who shot them. No one

saw anything. I always thought small towns were full of nosy people, and that anyone who is a stranger would stand out."

"Word has probably gotten around that you work for the FBI."

"I'm not here undercover. But people don't need to worry about me. They need to pay more attention to everyone else." She hugged her arms across her chest. "Did Todd say where he's staying now that he's checked out of the Nugget Inn?"

"No. I didn't ask. Guess I wasted your time, even calling to tell you he was here."

"No, you didn't waste my time." She moved to sit next to him on the sofa. Her floral scent distracted him, so he almost didn't hear her next words. "I'm frustrated. But that's not your fault. And I was planning on stopping by to see you this afternoon, anyway."

"Checking up on me?"

She didn't really have the face for fierceness, no matter how much she tried to pull it off. "I let my boss know about the man you saw outside the pub the night Judge Hennessey was murdered. I informed the sheriff, too. The FBI artist will be here tomorrow. You need to come into the sheriff's department and give your statement, then work with the artist to come up with a sketch of the man you saw the night Judge Hennessey was killed."

"I have a job," he said.

"This is more important."

"I already took off half of today to go on a Search and Rescue call. I can't take off again tomorrow."

"Come after work, then."

He didn't say anything, merely took another drink

of beer. She was wearing a blazer over her blouse, but he could see the silky black fabric of the top stretching over her breasts. He remembered how soft she had felt against him. How lithe and strong her body was. He didn't want to think about her that way, but he couldn't seem to stop himself.

"What was the Search and Rescue call?" she asked.

"A hiker broke her ankle. We had to hike up and bring her down on a litter."

"Was that hard?"

"Not really. Harder on her, I'm sure. As rescues go, it was pretty easy."

"What would she have done without you?"

"I'm not sure. It would have been about impossible to navigate that trail with a messed-up ankle."

She was looking at him differently now. That look made him uncomfortable "Do people realize how lucky they are to have volunteers like you who will drop everything and run to help them?" she asked.

"I'm not doing it to be anybody's hero," he said.

"There's no rule that says there's only one per family." She stood. "I'm starved. Have you eaten yet?"

What had she meant by the one-per-family remark? "My search and rescue work isn't about Camille," he said.

"Of course not. What do you have to eat?"

He followed her into the kitchen, where she opened the refrigerator and began pulling out produce and cheese. "If you have pasta, I can make a primavera," she said.

He opened a cabinet and took out a package of spaghetti. "Perfect."

He leaned back against the counter and watched as she set water to boil and pulled out a cutting board. "You like to cook," he said.

"Don't sound so surprised. My guilty pleasure is watching cooking shows."

"I don't think I have a guilty pleasure."

"No guilt, or no pleasure?"

Funny how one lift of her eyebrow could send heat curling through him. "No comment," he said and turned away, before he risked finding out how much pleasure—and guilt—she could offer him.

Chapter Fifteen

"We tracked Todd Arniston down at the Cakewalk Café this morning," Sheriff Walker told Shelby when she and the FBI artist met him at the sheriff's department the next afternoon. "He agreed to come in and talk to us. He answered our questions willingly, and he appears to be exactly what he says he is—a writer working on a book about the Chalk brothers."

"You should have called me in," she said.

"I would have if I thought there was a need," Walker said. "You're welcome to listen to the recording of the interview and read the transcripts. Arniston's story checked out. He doesn't have a criminal record, not even a traffic violation."

"He admits he was at the campground when Camille Gregory was murdered," she said.

"So were a lot of other people."

"Why didn't you interview him when you talked to the other campers?"

"He says he left the campground before floodwaters cut off the road. No one else mentioned him to us, and he didn't fill out a registration form for the campsite he occupied. But he doesn't deny being there. He says he didn't know Camille was there. No one else places him at or near her campsite."

"What about the stuffed bear that was left at Zach's townhouse?"

"We don't know when it was left there," Walker said. "It could have been any time between when Zach left for work that morning at eight until he returned home a little after nine at night. Arniston admits he can't account for his whereabouts for the entire thirteen hours, but most people wouldn't be able to. We didn't recover any fingerprints from the scene. Unless someone says they saw him or his car near Zach's townhouse, we don't have any reason to think he was responsible."

"He's been following Zach around."

"Because he wants to interview him," Walker said.

"Except he never said that until yesterday."

"I'll admit that's odd, but odd doesn't equal guilty."

"So you took everything he said at face value?" She couldn't keep the accusation from her voice.

The sheriff remained as unreadable as ever. "We took his fingerprints and sent them to the state for analysis," he said. "We'll let you know if anything turns up." He glanced toward the artist, who was setting up a laptop on a table in the interview room across the hall. "Has it occurred to you that Zach might have staged that bear in his townhouse? We only have his word that he lost his key."

"Zach did not stage that bear or lie about losing his key."

"People do that sort of thing in a bid for attention. How well do you really know him?"

I know him, she wanted to protest. She knew all of

Camille's stories about her brother—the quiet, thought-ful man who didn't go out of his way to seek attention. But stories weren't what counted with people like Sheriff Walker. "The FBI has a file on Zach Gregory that goes back more than four years," she said. "There are no signs of any tendency to lie or seek attention."

The sheriff glanced toward the FBI artist again. "He never told anyone about seeing someone outside the res-taurant the night that judge was murdered."

"Because he didn't think it was important, and he's not the type of man who likes to put himself forward."

Adelaide moved down the hallway toward them. "Zach Gregory is here," she said.

"I'll bring him back," Shelby said, and left before the sheriff could say anything else.

Zach stood at her approach. "What's wrong?" he asked.

"Nothing's wrong."

"You look angry about something."

She was tempted to tell him about the sheriff's ridic-ulous suggestion that he had made up the story about the bear, but decided against it. As much as she hated the idea of anyone suspecting Zach, she knew the sher-iff was approaching the case as any good law enforce-ment officer would, looking at everyone as a possible suspect. No matter how compelling the evidence, it was never a good idea to focus on only one suspect, espe-cially in the early stages of an investigation. "The art-ist is back here," she said. "You'll work with him first, then give your statement about what you saw that night at the restaurant. The artist will ask you questions about what you saw and use your answers to come up with a sketch, which you'll fine-tune together. The end result should be a drawing of the man you saw that night at the Britannia."

"What will you do while I'm doing that?" he asked.

"I have some calls to make. I'll check in with you soon."

She got Zach settled with the artist, an affable man named Fred who had driven over from Denver. "The most important thing is to relax and remember there are no wrong answers," he said as Shelby was leaving.

Though Sheriff Walker had offered her the use of an empty office in his department, she opted to walk outside to telephone Special Agent in Charge Lester. She told him about the sheriff's conclusions about Todd Arniston, and their inability to locate Janie.

"Neither of these people sound like very strong suspects to me," Lester said. "I don't think you're making enough progress in this case to justify keeping you in Eagle Mountain."

"Sir, I respectfully disagree. At least give me another day or two to follow some leads." She didn't have any leads to follow, but he didn't need to know that.

"I want you back in the office Monday morning, and that's final," he said.

"Yes, sir." She ended the call. Three days to find some kind of closure. Zach deserved that, even if it was the only thing she could give him.

ZACH SAT BACK and looked at the drawing on the artist's computer screen. A young man with a prominent nose and chiseled cheekbones looked out at him, fear haunting the man's dark eyes. For the space of a breath, Zach was back on that Houston street, the man silhouetted beneath the red glow of the traffic signal, his heart hammering in sympathy with the man's obvious terror.

"That's him," he said, back in the present now. "How did you do that?"

"You did it," Fred said. "I drew what you told me. I just knew the right questions to ask."

"Is it strange that I still remember him so well, after so much time has passed?"

"Not really. Trauma makes a strong impression. That, or a sense of connection with another person. You were afraid that night, and you saw that same feeling in him, even if you didn't acknowledge it." He started typing.

"What happens now?" Zach asked.

"I'll send this to my office, and from there it will be uploaded to various national databases. It will be up to the agents working the case, but sometimes these images are published in local media in the hopes that someone who recognizes the person will come forward." He closed the laptop. "You could help solve a crime. Or prevent another one."

He walked with Zach into the hallway, where Deputy Owen met him. "Come with me, and I'll take your statement," Owen said and led him into another interview room.

Telling the story yet again wasn't as difficult as Zach had anticipated. Declan Owen expressed no judgment or opinion, merely prompting Zach when he needed more detail or wanted to clarify the sequence of events. When Zach was done, he waited another quarter of an hour for a printed copy of his statement and signed it. "Thanks," Owen said. "You're free to go now."

He escorted Zach to the lobby, where he had expected to find Shelby waiting. Adelaide saw him looking around. "Agent Dryden said she would see you later," she said.

He hid his disappointment, but told himself he was being ridiculous. Hadn't he said he didn't want Shelby babysitting him? Maybe she felt the same way he did—that being together all the time was too frustrating, fighting this attraction between them, for reasons that still weren't clear to him. Though maybe she didn't want to start something she couldn't finish. He could understand that. She would need to go back to Houston sooner rather than later. The thought made him even more glum.

Rather than go home to mope, he stopped by Mo's, where he ordered nachos and a beer. He sat at a table by the window and watched groups of tourists on the sidewalk—couples and happy families laden with shopping bags, wearing souvenir T-shirts and stopping often to take pictures.

A flash of blond hair made him sit up straighter, and he leaned forward, studying a group of people across the street waiting to cross. Was that Janie in the back?

He shoved back his chair and rushed outside. But there was no tall blonde woman anywhere. He stood in the middle of the sidewalk, a boulder others had to move around, and stared in all directions.

Back in the restaurant, Kiki met him at the door. "Everything okay?" she asked.

"Yeah. I thought I saw someone I knew." He took out his wallet. "Let me settle up, and I'll get out of your hair."

He drove home, unable to relax. The tension didn't ease when he parked and saw someone by his door. He sat in the car, wondering if he should leave again, when Shelby moved into the light. He hurried to meet her. She didn't look happy to see him, fine lines of tension creasing her forehead. "We have to talk," she said.

As SOON AS the words were out of her mouth, Shelby silently cursed herself for being overly dramatic. Talk about a phrase that would send almost anyone running in the other direction. She rested a hand on his arm. "I just want to bring you up to date on some developments," she said.

"Sure." He unlocked the door, and she followed him in. They both stood just inside the door for a moment, looking around.

"Does everything look okay?" she asked.

"Sure. It's fine." He moved into the living room and sat on the sofa. "What's up?"

"I have to be back in Houston Monday."

Was that hurt or anger—or both—in his eyes? He didn't try to hide the emotions, merely shook his head. "I'm sorry to hear that," he said.

"The sheriff's department has agreed to run regular patrols, and if you see anything suspicious, they'll respond right away."

"I'm not sorry because I won't have a personal bodyguard anymore. I'm sorry because somehow, as awful as the past couple of weeks have been, you've made them bearable. Some parts of them have been good, even."

The kiss they had shared was good. She sat on the edge of the sofa, close but not touching. "I won't forget you, Zach."

"Yeah, you will. You'll always have another case. Another witness."

"You're not just another witness." He was Zach. Camille's brother. The man she had fallen for before they even met.

He didn't look away, his gaze challenging.

"I care about you, is that what you want me to say?" she asked.

"If that's true, why are you holding back?" he asked.

The problem was she wasn't holding back. Not the way she was supposed to, not letting herself get involved with people who were part of the cases she worked. "My problem is I can never be what I'm supposed to be," she said. "I'm not supposed to become friends with the witnesses or victims I interview. I'm not supposed to let my emotions get in the way of my objectivity. I'm not supposed to care. But I always care." She clenched her hands into fists. "I cared about Camille. She was my friend, and I miss her. And now I care about you."

He pulled her close, arms wrapped around her. "I know." When he looked into her eyes, she was sure he didn't see the cold FBI agent her bosses wanted her to be, but the warm woman whose feelings dictated her actions every bit as much as the evidence in a case.

She was growing warmer by the minute. She touched the tip of one finger to the corner of his mouth. "I'm not supposed to get involved with people who are part of my cases," she said. "I'm not supposed to be attracted to them."

He shifted, fitting her more firmly between his legs, the ridge of his erection pressed into her stomach. "You're not?" he asked, his voice gruff.

"I'm not." She raised up on her toes and replaced the finger on his mouth with her lips. "But I'm not a robot. I feel so much. I want you so much."

He moved his head just enough to cover her lips with his, his fingers buried in her hair, caressing the back of her neck, their bodies pressed together from chest to knee. He tasted of salt and beer, his lips so full and soft, his tongue warm and sensuous.

He broke the kiss and looked at her so long without speaking that her stomach fluttered with nerves. "What are you thinking?" she asked.

"That it's not wrong to care. And it isn't wrong to feel. And that professionalism is sometimes overrated."

Eyes still locked to hers, he slid one hand to her waist, then over the curve of her hip, down her thigh to the hem of her skirt. He pushed up the fabric, and she gasped at the heat of his palm on her bare skin. "Do you want me to stop?" he asked, lips close to her ear.

She shifted to look into his eyes again. "No."

He smiled, a lazy, sensuous expression that made her want to tear off his shirt. Instead, she settled for sliding her hand up under the fabric and across his taut stomach, his muscles contracting at her touch. "Do you want me to stop?" she asked, teasing.

"Not now. Not ever." He kissed her again, and she arched to him and hooked one leg around his thigh. He cupped her bottom, and she ground against him, while his mouth continued to prove that she only thought she had been kissed before. These were kisses she felt in every part of her. Was it possible, she wondered, to orgasm from a kiss?

"Let's go somewhere more comfortable," he said.

She nodded, and he led her to his bedroom. They were still moving toward the bed when he began to undress her, undoing buttons and lowering zippers with a minimum of fumbling. He peeled back her blouse and pressed his lips to the hollow of her shoulder, and she let out a sigh that was almost a purr and hooked one leg around his thigh to draw him closer.

He urged the blouse off her shoulders and down her arms, momentarily pinning her before she wriggled out. She popped the catch of her bra and cast it aside, then stepped back when he reached for her and took hold of the tab of his zipper. "You're still wearing too many clothes," she said.

For a big man, he moved quickly, and within seconds stood before her, naked in the glow of a single bedside lamp. He looked powerful, muscular and hairy chested. He might have been intimidating, but she felt safe with him. She wanted to touch every part of him and to feel him touch her.

"Do you have a condom?" she asked.

In answer, he opened the drawer of the bedside table and pulled out a foil packet. She smiled and moved into his arms.

He fell back on the bed and pulled her on top of him. He caressed her hip and smiled. "I was beginning to think this was never going to happen."

"Oh?" She straddled him, palms flat on his chest. "Have you been fantasizing about me?"

"All the time." He pulled her down and kissed her mouth, then began to work his way down her body.

She sighed again. "Do you like that?" he asked as he traced his tongue beneath her breasts.

"I do. And this." She moved his hand to cover her nipple.

"What about this?" she asked a few moments later, as she shifted against him.

"Oh, yeah," he said, and tucked her more securely against him. "And I like this view."

The men she had been with before hadn't talked much in bed. It wasn't that they ignored what she wanted—most were considerate lovers. But none took the time to check in with her the way Zach did. It surprised her, considering how quiet he was in everyday life. And it added another layer of connection she hadn't experienced before.

By the time he rolled on the condom and she welcomed him inside her, she felt tied to him more than physically. He held her gaze as the tension between them built, and when she felt herself on the edge, he kissed her with such tenderness tears stung her eyes, even as her body shuddered with passion. Then she felt his own release, moving through her, too.

Afterward, they lay curled together, silent, as if they had said everything that needed saying. She fought sleep, wanting this intense closeness to last as long as possible. But she must have drifted off anyway because the next thing she knew, Zach was shaking her. "Your phone is ringing," he said. "Do you need to answer it?"

She groaned, then sank back onto the pillows when the phone stopped ringing. But the message alert sounded almost immediately. "I'd better check," she said and struggled to a sitting position. She wrapped the sheet around her and made her way into the front room and retrieved her phone from her purse and carried it with her back into the bedroom.

Zach was sitting up now, too, blankets around his

hips. She stared for a moment, struck by the thought that she would never get tired of looking at this man naked. "Who called?" he asked.

She came out of her daze and looked at the phone. "The sheriff." Her heart sped up as she tapped in the code to access her voicemail.

As usual, Sheriff Walker didn't mince words. "Call me," he said.

She returned his call and waited while the phone rang once, twice...on the third ring, he picked up. "Where are you?" he asked.

"Why do you need to know that?"

"We just found Todd Arniston."

"Where did you find him?" And why did she care? Hadn't the sheriff already dismissed Todd as a suspect?

"We found him in a car parked on the road near the Piñon Creek campground. He was shot in the back of the head. He's dead."

She gasped, and Zach leaned toward her. "What is it?" he asked.

"I'll be right there," she said to the sheriff.

"There's something else you should know," Walker said. "We just got a report on the fingerprints we sent in. Todd Arniston wasn't his real name. His real name was Thomas Chalk."

Chapter Sixteen

Zach insisted on going with Shelby to the sheriff's department. The sheriff, dressed in jeans and a T-shirt, met them at the back of the dark building. He frowned at Zach, but didn't say anything and allowed him to follow Shelby to a cramped office. Zach settled into one of the two chairs facing the desk. Walker sat behind the desk and tapped the keyboard to wake up his computer.

"Thomas Chalk is Charlie and Christopher Chalk's nephew, is that right?" Shelby asked. "I remember the name from our files, but I can't recall anything about him."

"Great nephew," Walker said. "He's the grandson of their older brother, Carter Chalk."

"Carter isn't involved in the family businesses," Shelby said. She turned to Zach. "Carter made a point of cutting himself off from the rest of the family as soon as he was out of college. He operates a ranch in Wyoming and, as far as we've been able to determine, has no involvement with any of their affairs."

"There's more," Walker said. "Thomas has an older brother, Martin." He angled the computer screen toward them to show a photograph of a dark-haired young man with a prominent nose.

Gooseflesh rose on Zach's arms. "That's the man I saw outside the Britannia Pub the night the judge was killed," he said.

"You're sure?" Walker asked.

"Yes, I'm sure."

"Martin Chalk is dead," Shelby said. "I remember now. He drowned six months after Judge Hennessey was killed, before Charlie and Christopher's trial. It was ruled an accidental death."

Zach sat back, trying to sort out the thoughts spinning in his head. "Do you think Martin was killed to silence him about whatever he saw at the restaurant that night?"

"His death was never investigated as a possible murder," Shelby said. "I'd have to review the file, but the only mention I remember seeing was that he died in an accident when his boat was swamped on a lake where he was fishing, and that he had nothing to do with the Chalk brothers' crimes."

"Why was Thomas Chalk here?" Zach asked. "Did he kill Camille?"

"We sent his hair to the FBI lab to see if it matches the one you found at the campsite," Travis said. He turned the computer monitor back to face him and typed. "Now take a look at this photo." He turned the monitor again, this time to show a photo of a beautiful blonde.

"That's Janie!" Both Shelby and Zach spoke. He leaned closer, but there was no mistaking the woman in this photo for anyone other than the woman who had pursued him.

"Her name is Janelle Chalk," Travis said. "She's Thomas's twin sister."

ZACH TRIED TO focus on the road on this short drive to Shelby's hotel room, where she wanted to retrieve her laptop and files. But everything Travis and Shelby had told him kept pulling his thoughts away. "What were Janelle and her brother doing here?" he asked. "Did they kill Camille? Were they stalking me or something? And why?"

"Maybe they found out you saw their brother at the pub that night," Shelby said.

"But what difference does that make if their brother is dead?"

"I don't know." She stared at her phone, typing furiously. "I'm trying to log into my files at the Bureau, but the system isn't exactly set up to be read on a phone screen." She laid the phone in her lap. "I texted my boss with the news about the twins, though I don't know if he'll read the message tonight."

"You said they aren't involved in the Chalk brothers' crimes."

"Not that we know of. But maybe that's changed."

"Maybe Martin was at the pub that night to try to stop the killing," Zach said. "He got frightened and ran away."

"Or maybe he was the killer," Shelby said. "Maybe the Chalk brothers were right, and they didn't pull the trigger after all. Though that doesn't mean they didn't orchestrate the whole thing. Maybe Martin wanted in on the action, and killing the judge was the price of admission."

"Then why kill him six months later?"

"Maybe his death really was an accident. Or maybe he got cold feet and threatened to turn himself in. Or

Charlie and Christopher were afraid he would cave under pressure and decided to eliminate the risk."

"So what were Thomas and Janelle doing in Eagle Mountain? Were they following Camille?"

"Or they were here to kill you," she said. "Maybe that's what led Camille here. I don't know. But we'll do our best to find out."

At the motel, Shelby fired up her laptop and scrolled through her files. Zach couldn't sit still, so he paced, mind and heart racing. "Where is Janelle now?" he wondered. "Is she hiding from whoever killed her brother? Or did she kill him?"

Shelby shook her head. "My files have almost nothing on those two. They're on a list of Chalk relatives, but as far as the FBI knows, they're both living quiet lives in Wyoming. This says that Thomas works on the ranch with his father and Janelle is a dental hygienist." She glanced up at him. "They both sound so ordinary."

"I wasn't really worried before," he said. "But now I feel like I'm waiting for the next terrible thing to happen. And I know the sheriff said he had contacted the police in Junction about protecting my parents, but maybe I should go to them."

"That wouldn't be a bad idea," she said. "It would get you away from here, someplace safer and with a law enforcement presence twenty-four hours a day."

"What will you do?" he asked. "Do you still have to be in Houston Monday?"

"I don't know. I would think this would change things." She closed the laptop. "Let's go back to your place. You can pack to go to your folks while I keep trying to get more information on the Chalk twins."

It probably would have been easier for her to stay at the motel and work alone, but he appreciated that they would be together a little while longer. He took her hand as they walked out to his car. "I'm going to miss you while I'm gone," he said.

"I'm going to miss you, too." She leaned against him. "But I promise, we'll talk every day."

And what about when this is all over? he wondered, but didn't dare ask out loud. What about when she went back to Houston, and he tried to settle in once more to life here in Eagle Mountain? Would they try to keep up a long-distance relationship, something that seemed to him doomed to fail? Or would they part as friends? The idea made his chest hurt. Better not to dwell on that uncertain future. He needed all his attention on now.

He parked in the lot in front of his townhouse and led the way down the path to his front door. But when he tried his key in the lock, it wouldn't go in.

"What's wrong?" Shelby asked.

"The key won't go in. It's like something is jamming the lock." He leaned down for a closer look but was unable to make out anything in the dim light.

A gasp from Shelby made him look up.

Janie—or rather Janelle Chalk—smiled at him. She held a pistol pressed to Shelby's side. "Don't try anything," Janelle said. "Or I'll kill her, then finish you off."

SHELBY TRIED TO remember the self-defense training she had received earlier in her career: How to overpower an opponent. How to evade capture. How to use your opponent's weaknesses against them. But none of those lessons applied here, with the barrel of a pistol pressed hard against her ribs and Zach standing across from her, his face bleached of color and eyes filled with horror.

Janelle patted her down and found Shelby's pistol and pocketed it. "Get back in your car," she ordered, grabbing Shelby's arm and marching her forward, the gun between them. She wore black pants and a black hoodie, the hood pulled up to hide her blond hair. She had a small black daypack on her back. Anyone seeing her would describe a tall, slim figure—the same description the camper had given the sheriff of the "man" he had seen running from Camille's campsite the day she died. "You drive, Zach," Janelle said. "But remember what will happen if you start thinking you're smarter than I am."

"Where are we going?" Zach asked as he opened the driver's door of his truck.

Janelle led Shelby to the passenger side and shoved her in. Shelby was grateful for Zach's bulk beside her, somehow comforting. Of course, it also meant that if Janelle decided to fire the pistol in these close quarters, both she and Zach were likely to be hurt. "Where do you want me to drive?" Zach asked again as Janelle shut the door behind her.

"Go to the Piñon Creek campground. I think it's fitting, don't you, that we end everything there."

The small town of Eagle Mountain was so much darker than Houston at night, without thousands of streetlights, traffic lights and the glow from homes and towering office buildings shutting out the night. But away from town, on the Forest Service road, they were plunged into a new kind of darkness. The headlights of Zach's truck cut a narrow wedge out of the inky blackness, revealing nothing but closely growing trees and the narrow strip of red dirt road directly in front of them.

Zach drove slowly, clutching the steering wheel in both hands as if he might rip it from the column. He stared straight ahead, and Shelby wondered what he was thinking. Her own mind raced, searching for some avenue of escape. But shaping a coherent thought was liking extracting bolts from a vat of molasses. The effort drained her, and nothing she could assemble made sense.

"What are you doing here in Eagle Mountain?" Zach asked, breaking the silence and making Shelby jump. "Did you come with your brother?"

"I followed him here because I knew he was going to screw up," Janelle said. "Not that he minded me being here. I've always been the only one of us with any real backbone. He just went along with Uncle Charlie and Uncle Christopher because he was afraid of them."

"What was he doing here, then?" Zach asked. "Was he really writing a book about the Chalk brothers?"

Janelle laughed. "No, he wasn't writing a book! That was just a story he made up to get close to you. He had this idea that we should find out what you really knew about what happened that night at the pub before we killed you. I told him it didn't matter what you knew because the uncles wanted you dead, but Thomas felt he had to know if the killing was justified. He actually said that. As if it matters."

The casual way she spoke, as if murder was a mundane topic of conversation, sent an icy chill through Shelby. "I saw your brother, Martin, running away from the pub that night," Zach said.

"I knew it!" Janelle looked around Shelby to smile at

him. "Martin told us there was a truck parked in front of the restaurant that night. He thought it was empty, but I was sure you were there, waiting on your sister. Of course, no one would listen to me for the longest time. After all, I'm just a girl." The smile turned to a sneer. "My uncles wasted so much time focused on Martin and Thomas, even though I was right there—the only one with guts enough to have a real role in the family organization. But because I'm female, I have to work so much harder to prove I'm capable. All my brothers had to do was stand around looking the part, when neither one of them had the nerve to actually do the work necessary."

"Martin looked really afraid the night I saw him," Zach asked. "What was he doing at the pub?"

"He was terrified," Janelle said. "All he had to do was show up, fire one shot into that worthless judge and Charlie and Christopher were going to hand over a whole chunk of their empire. Legitimate businesses, most of them. He would have been rich. Instead, as soon as he shot the judge, he fell apart. He ran away like the coward he was, all the way back to Wyoming. He told my uncles he had changed his mind and wanted to stay on the ranch. He promised not to say anything about what happened that night, but they couldn't trust him. How could they? He was liable to fall apart the first time anyone came to question him." She turned to Shelby. "But you never did. The FBI never figured out there was someone else in the pub that night, even when Charlie and Christopher's attorneys kept insisting my uncles never fired a shot. They told the truth."

"Why didn't your uncles tell the authorities that Martin killed the judge?" Zach said. "Especially if he wasn't around to implicate them?"

"Family loyalty and the family name are everything to them," Janelle said. "It's why they were so keen on getting my brothers involved. The two of them only have daughters. One of them has never married, and the other is a lesbian. They figured if they were going to find a man to run things when they decided to retire, my brothers were the best candidates. They couldn't see that I was the one they really needed."

Silence wrapped around them, broken only by the crunch of the truck's tires on the dirt road. Shelby watched Janelle out of the corner of her eye. The other woman was smiling slightly. She looked so pleased with herself.

"Who killed Thomas?" Zach asked after a moment.

"He couldn't follow through on the job he was sent here to do, and he was becoming a liability," Janelle said.

"So you shot him?" Shelby asked.

Janelle's look was withering. "I did what I had to do," she said.

"Did you kill Camille, too?" Zach asked.

"I did. But I promise, she didn't suffer. She wasn't even supposed to be here, but she must have found out what Thomas and I had planned and came here to warn you. Under different circumstances, the two of us might have been friends. I always felt she was a strong woman, like me." She leaned forward a little. "Your turn should be coming up soon. The sign can be hard to see."

A few minutes later, the headlights illuminated the brown Forest Service sign that identified the campground. "Turn in and drive to the back," Janelle ordered. "Stop at number 47."

The campsite where Camille had been killed. "Is this where you killed Thomas, too?" Shelby asked.

"It is. The sheriff will have moved his car and his body by now. I like the symmetry of having everything take place here. I hope my uncles appreciate it."

Zach turned into the campground and bumped along the rutted road, past parked vans, RVs and tents set up next to stunted trees and stone fire rings.

Yellow crime-scene tape still fluttered from the last campsite on the road, and the broken tree still lay across the parking area. Zach pulled alongside the tree and cut the engine. The lights remained on, shining into the darkness. "If you shoot us here, the campers will hear," Zach said.

"There's no cell service here," she said. "By the time they call for help, I'll be long gone. I left my car in another campsite nearby. With a tent set up and everything. So the other campers probably think I'm sleeping. I hitchhiked to your place. It's not hard for a woman who looks like me to get a ride." She opened the passenger door. "Get out. We're going to take a little walk. And remember, if you try anything, I'm not going to miss at this range."

Zach squeezed Shelby's arm as she started to slide across the seat away from him. She glanced back at him, but couldn't read his expression in the darkness. "Go on," he whispered.

She wanted to tell him to run. She would distract Janelle and probably die in the process. But Zach could disappear into the darkness and would have a chance of getting away.

"Come out on this side, Zach," Janelle said. "I don't want you out of my sight."

He maneuvered his big frame awkwardly over the center console of the truck and joined them beside the vehicle. The headlights blinked off and darkness surrounded them. They could use the darkness to their advantage, Shelby thought. If they could get even a few feet away from Janelle, she wouldn't be able to see well enough to hit them.

And then what? They could try to get help from one of the campers, and possibly involve innocent bystanders in a firefight. They could run, but where? From what she remembered from her visits in the daytime, the area around the campground was a wooded mountainside along the river, full of uneven terrain, fallen trees, loose rock and other hazards. For all her law enforcement training, she had spent most of her career patrolling, interviewing, researching and compiling reports. She didn't feel prepared for a situation like this.

ZACH'S MIND RACED through all the possibilities in their situation. They were at the very back of the campground, away from most of the campers. In the darkness, he had only noticed a few sites occupied, and at this hour most people would be sleeping. He could hear the murmur of the river to their right. The terrain beyond the campground was rugged woods, scattered boulders and fallen trees from the recent storm ready to trip up anyone trying to flee in the darkness. If they did succeed in breaking free, they would have to run a long way before they got to a place where they could call for help.

They had darkness and numbers in their favor, but the pistol in Janelle's hand and her determination to use it evened the odds, or put them in her favor. He could try to distract her and allow Shelby to get away. He would probably be wounded or killed. And then what? Janelle would go after Shelby. Shelby was from the city. She didn't know the terrain around here. He didn't like her chances alone in this remote area with a killer after her.

He had to keep Janelle talking. As long as she was talking to them, they would still be alive. "Do your uncles know you're here, doing this for them?" he asked.

"They think I'm back home on the ranch where I belong." Bitterness colored her words. "When they find out I've accomplished what my brothers couldn't, they'll see me in a new light."

Zach eased one step back, moving as soundlessly as possible. Every foot away from her would make it harder for her to see him and easier for him to make a break if he got the chance.

"Come over here closer to me." She gestured with the pistol. "I don't trust you. You're probably thinking you're a big guy. You could overpower me. But I won't hesitate to shoot, and I'm a very good shot. There's not a lot for me to do on the ranch but practice."

Reluctantly, he did as she asked, moving not only closer to her, but to Shelby. He would do all he could to keep her safe. Keeping the gun aimed at him, she turned to Shelby. "Get some of the police tape that's around the campsite and tie up Zach," she said. "Ankles and wrists. And remember, if you try to run or scream or do anything suspicious, he dies."

Shelby turned toward the road. "How am I going to see what I'm doing?" she asked. "Even with the moon, it's so dark."

Janelle shifted and slipped her pack off her back. "Look in there, and you'll find a flashlight."

Shelby opened the pack and, after a few seconds, drew out a small flashlight.

"Give it to Zach," Janelle said. "Zach, you keep the light on her. I'll keep the gun on you."

Shelby's fingers brushed his as she handed him the light. They were ice-cold. Then she moved away, toward the tape strung on the far side of the camp.

The light was small, not heavy enough to use as a club. He trained the beam on Shelby. A powerful blue-tinged glow cut through the blackness. There was another campsite directly across from this one, but it was empty.

Zach shifted his stance and the back of his heel struck something solid. The broken tree. He pictured it in his mind, five inches across and shattered into two pieces. Could he pick up one of the pieces and use it as a club? He thought he could do it. Could he knock Janelle off-balance before she shot him? At this range, one shot could be deadly.

"Do you have a knife or scissors?" Shelby asked, her voice sounding loud in the stillness. "I can't undo these knots, and this stuff is designed to not tear."

"Keep working at it," Janelle called. "I'm not going to hand you anything that could be used as a weapon."

Keep her talking, Zach thought. *Keep her distracted.*

Shelby grunted and tugged hard on the tape. "It's not coming loose," she called.

"That's because you're making the knots tighter," Janelle said. "If you keep being difficult, I'm just going to go ahead and shoot you." She was frowning in Shelby's direction, and though the pistol still pointed at Zach, the barrel had dropped slightly. He swung the light up, aiming for her eyes, the brilliant light blinding her.

Janelle swore and put up a hand to shield her eyes. Zach bent and hefted the log. The gun went off, the bullet striking the log in his hand, the impact forcing him to take a step back to regain his balance. But he recovered quickly and swung the log at Janelle, aiming for her head and shoulders.

The impact of the heavy wood striking flesh and bone shuddered through him. Janelle screamed, and the gun went off again, then she crumpled to the ground. He dropped the log and retrieved the flashlight from the ground.

Shelby ran to him and scooped up the gun Janelle had dropped. They stood for a moment, staring down at the woman on the ground. She was curled in a fetal position, moaning.

"Hey! What's going on over there!"

Zach directed the light toward the sound and saw a man in shorts and sandals standing in the road. Shelby moved toward him. "I'm with the FBI," she called. "Please drive until you get a cell signal and call 911. We're going to need the sheriff and an ambulance."

The man hesitated, staring. "Go!" Shelby urged. "Please. It's important."

He nodded and ran back down the road. Zach knelt beside Janelle and felt at her throat for a pulse. She opened her eyes. "I think you broke my shoulder," she said.

"It will heal," he said. "Lie still. The ambulance will be here soon."

She groaned and closed her eyes again.

Shelby came to stand beside him. "I can't believe I was wrong about everything," she said. "The Chalk brothers didn't kill the judge or your sister."

Zach put an arm around her and pulled her close. "They orchestrated the judge's killing and ordered Camille killed, too," he said. "That makes them responsible."

She continued to stare at Janelle. "She killed her own brother. That's so horrible."

"It is. But it's over now."

She glanced at him. "Is it? The Chalk brothers will say they didn't know anything about this. They're very good at making people believe them."

He blew out a breath. Was she right? "Let's just focus on now," he said. "We're safe. We're together. That's all I want to think about." That was all that really mattered, wasn't it?

Chapter Seventeen

Shelby's eyelids felt as if they were lined with sand-paper, and her mouth tasted like old socks soaked in bad coffee. She sat in an interview room at the Rayford County Sheriff's Department, across from Special Agent in Charge Lester, who had arrived at dawn with a team of federal marshals who took custody of Janelle Chalk. She hadn't slept in more than twenty-four hours and wasn't sure what time it was now—probably before nine in the morning. All she wanted was a shower and to crawl into bed, preferably with Zach, whom she hadn't seen since they had arrived at the sheriff's department in separate vehicles hours ago.

She had spent most of the hours since then giving her statement to Sheriff Walker, then repeating the story for Lester. Her account of Janelle's statements about the judge's death, and the admission that Janelle had murdered both Camille and her brother, had sharpened his attention, and he had her repeat everything twice.

"Zach Gregory's sighting of Martin Chalk outside the pub that night confirms that Martin was at the scene," Lester said. "But Janelle is refusing to say anything now that she's in custody."

"Zach heard the same thing I did," Shelby said. "He'll confirm my story."

"And Charlie and Christopher will deny having anything to do with her and her brothers," Lester said.

"We can find more evidence," she said. "We can make a case against them. Especially if we can persuade Janelle to talk. She might do it if we promise her a deal."

"*We* will not be doing anything," he said. "I'm removing you from the case."

The shock of this statement cut through her fatigue. "Why?"

Lester's expression was grim. "For one thing, I understand you've become personally involved with Zach Gregory."

She opened her mouth to protest, but what could she say? She couldn't deny her feelings for Zach. "I know how to keep my personal and private lives separate," she said. "And it's not as if I'm involved with a member of the Chalk family."

"You're being reassigned. And you're booked on a one o'clock flight back to Houston." He checked his watch. "You should have just enough time to change clothes, gather your belongings and get to the airport."

"I'd like to see Zach before I leave."

"That isn't possible."

"Why not?" Alarm jolted through her. "Is something wrong? Is he all right?"

"Zach and his parents are going into witness security as of right now. Practically the first words out of Janelle Chalk's mouth when we spoke to her were that her uncles would wipe out the Gregory family in revenge for Zach hurting her."

"I'm not sure she's as valuable to her uncles as she believes she is," Shelby said.

"Nevertheless, we feel the danger to the Gregorys is real, and they have agreed to accept our help."

Zach was going away. Just like that. "I want to see him," she said. "I need to say goodbye."

"It would be better for everyone if you didn't." Lester stood. "Agent Crispin will drive you to your hotel to collect your things, then to the airport. We'll talk again next week."

He left the room without a backward glance. Agent Crispin, who had been standing by the door, walked over to her. He was a man in his late thirties, with short dark hair and chiseled features. The type of agent portrayed on recruiting posters, never a hair out of place or a move out of line. "Come on," he said. "You don't want to miss your plane."

She thought of telling him to get lost. She wasn't a prisoner. She could refuse to get on that plane, refuse to return to work.

And then what? She'd be out of a job, stuck miles from home and Zach would still be gone. She knew how witness security worked. Once the decision was made, few people looked back. The important thing was to keep Zach and his family safe. She couldn't do anything to compromise his safety. Even if it meant breaking her heart.

She waited until she was in the shower at the motel before she let herself cry. But she pulled herself together by the time she met up with Agent Crispin again. "You'll probably get a commendation for this, you know?" Crispin said as they headed to the airport. "What you did, capturing Janelle Chalk, took all kinds of guts."

Zach did it, she thought. He was the one who swung that log and hit Janelle, even as she was shooting at him. Without him, they might both be dead. But she didn't say that to Crispin. Talking about Zach hurt too much. She needed to find a way to lock that grief away so that she could still function. She had so much work to do.

Nine months later

MIKE CLAUDE DUG crampons into the ice coating the ledge on which he and fellow Search and Rescue volunteer Dave Mitchell stood. He clung to a rope with one hand and looked over his shoulder at the car that lay on its side on the edge of Cub Creek. A motorist had seen the dark gray sedan hit a patch of ice on the highway above and skid over the cliff and had called 911. Mike had just reported for work when he got the text and headed for Search and Rescue headquarters.

"From here, it's just a short drop to that clear section of gravel behind the vehicle." Dave pointed to a spot about fifteen feet below them. "We should be able to secure the vehicle to those trees over there."

"Looks good," Mike said. "I'm ready when you are."

Dave was right—the rappel down was short and easy. Mike was getting more comfortable with the rope work. He had spent a lot of hours these past nine months climbing, both in the gym and outdoors. It was a good way to let off steam and gave him time to process all the changes in his life. The new name, for instance. He was getting used to thinking of himself as Mike, not Zach. He was from the Midwest, newly relocated to northern

California, working for a solar energy company. That was his reality now, and he was coming to accept it.

He and Dave secured the vehicle and determined it contained a lone woman driver. She was responsive, though in pain and frightened, trapped in the vehicle, on her back in the collapsed driver's seat, the powder from the exploded airbag coating her like frost. "We're going to take care of you, ma'am," Mike reassured her. "Just stay still, and we'll have you out in no time."

Darcy Yates, a paramedic, and Dr. Tim Westmoreland arrived minutes later. Darcy, a petite woman with short, dark hair, climbed in through a busted window and began assessing the woman's injuries and keeping her as calm and as protected as possible while Mike and Dave began cutting apart the sedan.

Less than ten minutes later, the four of them worked together to transfer the woman—Marian—to a backboard and litter. They maneuvered her out of the vehicle to the ground, then prepared to haul her up. More volunteers arrived to help, and thirty minutes later, Marian was being loaded into a helicopter that had landed in the middle of the highway. The helicopter rose up and away. The volunteers watched it go, then turned away and began to clean up and gather equipment.

"Great job, Mike." Captain Ray Valdez clapped him on the back. "We're glad to have you with us."

"Glad I can help," he said. Being part of a Search and Rescue group helped him feel comfortable with this new life. That, and knowing his parents were safe.

His mom and dad—now Bill and Sally Claude— seemed to be enjoying their new life. "It's kind of nice, starting over," his mother had confided. "We're never going to forget Camille, but it's good to try to build a new life now. One that isn't connected to the Chalk brothers and everything that happened."

Except that Mike would always be connected to that.

In the early months, he had thought about little else, replaying that night over and over and over again. The last night he had seen Shelby. When he had asked to see her after his interviews with the sheriff and the FBI, he had been told she had already left to fly back to Houston. The news had stunned him. She hadn't even bothered to say goodbye? The FBI agent, a woman named Rochelle, must have seen his confusion. "She knows you're going into witness protection," she said, her voice gentle. "That's hard enough without prolonging the goodbyes."

They hadn't been together long. He told himself he would get over her soon enough. Except that hadn't happened. He was doing well, rebuilding his life into something better than ever. But there was still an ache when he thought of Shelby. She had meant something to him, and then she was simply gone.

He helped unload the gear at SAR headquarters, then went with Dave and the others for pizza and beer. He was trying to do that more, to be more social and part of the group. He had thought it would be difficult, remembering to give them the background story the Marshals Service had helped him compose to go with his new identity. But he had learned pretty quickly that almost no one asked about his past. They didn't really care.

As for the Chalk brothers, he hadn't heard anything from them. He checked the internet for news of them sometimes, but nothing came up. Janelle Chalk had been charged with the murder of Camille Gregory and Todd

Chalk and was awaiting trial, but he hadn't been able to find out anything more. Rochelle had visited once and told him she didn't think he would have to testify in Janelle's trial. "We have enough evidence without exposing you," she had said.

He had asked her about Shelby, and she shut him down. "I can't tell you anything," she had said and turned away.

He tried to tell himself it didn't matter. He and his parents were safe. One day, he might even be happy again.

He left the pizza place and drove to the bungalow he was buying on a quiet street on the west side of town. He pulled into the driveway and cut the lights, then sat for a moment, studying the house with its little front porch and brick pillars.

Then a movement on the edge of the light made his heart stop. A woman stood there, silhouetted in the moonlight, a slight figure with hair around her shoulders. Not Janelle Chalk. This woman wasn't that tall. But Janelle might have cousins. Other Chalk women who saw themselves as assassins.

He started the car again, thinking he would drive away. He'd call his contact at the Marshals Service. Then the woman hurried down the steps toward him. "Zach, don't go," she said. "It's me. Shelby."

He didn't remember getting out of the car. He didn't remember running to her or pulling her close. But there they were, clinging to each other, both their faces wet with tears. He pulled her into the house and turned on the lights. "Let me look at you," he said. "I can't believe this is real." Maybe it was just another dream. One where he held her and loved her, only to wake to find her gone.

"It's real," she said, tightening her arms around him.

She was thinner than he remembered, her hair longer and a little darker. "I'm sorry it took me so long to get to you," she said. "I had to wait until you were settled in your new identity, and then it took some detective work to find you."

"My name is Mike now," he said. "Mike Claude."

"I know." She smiled, and he felt as if he'd stepped out of heavy metal armor that had been binding him for nine months.

"How did you find me?" he asked. "No one is supposed to be able to do that."

"I had help," she said. "Do you remember me talking about Phil?"

"Phil?" He shook his head. "I don't remember."

"The marshal Camille was in love with."

"The man who was ordered away and didn't come back?" He didn't have a lot of good thoughts about that man.

"He always regretted choosing his job over Camille. He agreed to help me find you, but he had to be careful. It took a while."

She caressed the side of his face. "It doesn't matter. I'm here now."

She leaned in as if to kiss him, but he turned his head to the side. "What happened? Why didn't I see you again the night we captured Janelle?"

"My boss wasn't happy about our relationship. He told me you were going into witness security and I would never see you again. Then he ordered me on a plane back to Houston. I started to refuse, but knew that would mean quitting my job and losing my best chance of finding you again."

He looked into her eyes, hers still glistening with tears.

"I was determined to see you again. I'm just sorry you had to wait so long."

"Are you still with the FBI?"

"No."

"What are you going to do?"

"I don't know. But I'll find a job. Somewhere close. That is, if you still want us to be together." Her arms around him loosened. "A lot can happen in nine months. Maybe you've changed your mind."

He pulled her against him once more. "I haven't changed my mind. I thought about looking for you, too, but I didn't know where to start. I looked online, but couldn't find anything."

"It's not a great idea for an FBI agent to have an on-line presence," she said. "And my address and phone number are confidential, too."

"I thought I'd lost you." His voice broke on the last word.

"You never lost me. And I'm here now."

He had always said he didn't believe in fate or destiny or anything like that. Too much of what happened to people in life happened by accident. Camille always said she was at the pub the night Judge Hennessey was killed because she was meant to bring the Chalk brothers to justice. But that hadn't happened. She had merely been at the wrong place at the wrong time, and that hadn't worked out well for any of them. Their family had lost everything, even their names.

But he had found Shelby. Or rather, she had found him. He looked into her eyes. "I love you," he said.

"I love you, too. It's a little scary sometimes, how much. I think I fell in love with you listening to all the stories Camille told about you. I fell in love with the idea of you, then when we met, the reality was even better than the fantasy. How could I not love you?"

"I fell in love with you the night you brought over pizza," he said. "I was more than halfway there before then, but that night sealed the deal."

"Because of that kiss?" she asked.

"Because you put mushrooms on the pizza."

She looked puzzled. "But you don't like mushrooms."

"Exactly. You didn't feel like you had to leave them off the pizza just because I didn't want them. I liked that. I liked that you were sure of yourself that way. That you didn't try to make yourself over to please someone else. I felt like when I was with you, I was getting the real you, and that's who I fell in love with."

"Mike?"

"Mmm?"

"I've been practicing saying the name. I'm getting used to it."

"I'm still figuring out this new life."

"I hope you'll let me be a part of it."

"I never wanted to do it without you."

They kissed again, and for a long time neither said anything. It was enough to know that no matter what the future brought, they would face it together.

* * * * *

*Look for more books in Cindi Myers's
Eagle Mountain: Criminal History miniseries,
coming soon, only from Harlequin Intrigue!*